Night of the Cat

Night of the Cat

James Schermerhorn

St. Martin's Press
New York

Production Editor: David Stanford Burr

Library of Congress Cataloging-in-Publication Data

Schermerhorn, James.
    Night of the cat / James Schermerhorn.
        p. cm.
    "A Thomas Dunne book."
    ISBN 0-312-09887-1
    1. Policewomen—California—San Francisco—Fiction. 2. San Francisco (Calif.)—Fiction. I. Title.
PS3569.C48433N54 1993
813′.54—dc20   93-11467
                                CIP

First Edition: October 1993

10 9 8 7 6 5 4 3 2 1

This book is
dedicated to

Matthew Schuyler,
Katherine Park,
and
James IV

In the order of their appearance.

And to the next generation,

Anna Rose
and
Jessica Swan

Who arrived almost hand in hand.

I hope many people will find here police officers they have known. It will not be true, but I'll be pleased if the men and women in my book ring true. I've known police all my life—as a child, when they watched over me on paper routes in Birmingham, Michigan, even earlier when I napped on a cracked leather couch on the police beat in Detroit, where first my father, James Schermerhorn, Jr., then his younger cousin, Jack Schermerhorn, worked for the *Detroit News* and the *Detroit Free Press*. My father, in those years, was writing adventure novels for the young, *The Mystery Ship of Boca Ciga Bay* and others, published by Dodd, Mead & Co. And my own forty years in California, working for the *Santa Barbara News-Press* and the *Examiner* in San Francisco.

Night of the Cat was vetted for me by Commander Ray Canepa, in charge of the city's uniformed police in San Francisco, and by Sergeant Ted Bell, who still works in the Taraval police district along the city's ocean beaches. I thank them both. The errors, however, are my own.

—James Schermerhorn

Night of the Cat

Prologue

August 5

The two men didn't fit in the tree-lined San Francisco neighborhood with its rectangles of neat lawns and trimmed gardens, the curbs empty here, the cars parked down long shaded driveways or behind locked garage doors.

Large men, they wore sport coats, one a modest herringbone, the other a broad plaid. They wore shirts and ties, but they weren't salesmen. They weren't building inspectors. They didn't live here, but they didn't shuffle their feet in their solid-looking shoes either.

A knowledgeable person would have glanced from the shoes to the bulges at the back of their jackets. One bulge on each was the handcuffs, the other a gun. They were police. They belonged.

In an even richer neighborhood they might call at the

back door. Here they had parked at the curb, walked past the tall privet hedge and up the stone walk between the blooming impatiens and flaring oleander to dwarf the secluded front stoop. The smaller one pushed the bell.

There were no warning footsteps through the house. The door was opened partway, then held firmly by a woman with a lean face framed in short dark hair, a silk dress, gold bracelets on tennis-tanned arms, an angry woman.

"You can't see her! I don't care what the doctor said! He did not have my permission!"

The big one in the plaid jacket said, "Inspector Mc-Kitrick. I talked to your mother an hour ago. Before you got here. She's expecting us. You're the daughter?"

She nodded but didn't step back from the doorway.

"This is Inspector Gallina. We're just going to sit with her while the department artist does his tricks. Standard procedure."

"Not here it isn't!"

"We've explained to her. She understands. She's expecting us." The smaller one spoke but the woman kept her eyes on McKitrick.

"It's not standard in this house!" she said. She was visibly trembling. "Not another newspaper story about the rape of a helpless old woman on Locust Street! It's not rape, you can't call it that! We're not charging that!" Each sentence pronounced now with trembling fury. "My husband said we will charge assault and nothing more. You'd better understand that, because I won't have any more newspaper stories I'll have to face down. I don't have to put up with that!"

Gallina's voice didn't boom like McKitrick's. "The medical evidence tells us what happened. It's very clear.

2

We'll go over it with you if you want us to. Now we just want his picture. She knows that. She wants to be helpful. We'd like to find him before he does this to somebody else."

"I don't care what he does to somebody else!"

Her fury had no effect on them. They stood and waited. Defeated, she moved back and McKitrick stepped through the door. He said, "The department artist will be here in a minute. I'll get the door."

"I'll get the door here!" she said.

"We'll go back then," McKitrick said. "We know the way." He walked past her down the long hall lined with English prints and framed snapshots of grandchildren to the sunlit rear bedroom that looked out on a peaceful garden. The beautiful woman propped up in bed had a slim, serene face and white hair, and her smile was gracious when he tapped at the doorjamb and stepped into the room. She held a pale hand to hide the bruises at her throat. A pleasant nurse was hovering near yet she said she had no memory yet of anything that had happened to her.

August 6

Sex Crimes Inspector Florence Hendry started with a victim who did remember something. But how much?

She watched the woman with lank, thinning, dyed black hair bent over the flat drawing book of the department artist, John Carruthers, her hands reaching out to snatch it from disaster as it slithered along the counterpane, threatening to drop onto the floor. His young blond head was next to hers. She had a bandaged throat where she'd been bitten. She wasn't aware she was getting a full dose of therapy, Hendry thought. John Carruthers's therapy. He said, "We're missing a nose and an ear. They're here somewhere. There, can you shift that nose over here with your other hand?"

The older woman laughed hoarsely.

"Oh, that's right. You've only got two. Well, here, I've got one I'm not using, I don't think." He reached across and pulled over a drawing, propped it on the counterpane. "There. That's the one. Isn't it?"

"That's it. More the bent skinny one. He got it caught in a wringer." She looked up at Hendry and laughed again, hoarsely.

We give therapy, Hendry said to herself. One old female policewoman and one young talented cop who'd rather draw pictures than tear around on the midnight watch wrecking radio cars.

For fifteen minutes she'd watched fear giving way to a fascination with this young officer and his drawing project.

"Now, are we getting it? Here. I need that chin. That one." She slithered the paper over, turned it right side up. "Good. Now I'll put it right here where a chin ought to be, then we'll have to do the mouth. You still haven't found the right mouth."

"That's the hardest part," the old woman croaked. "It was always open, and he was snarling, you know. I just saw it all pink and white and slimy with his tongue and his teeth. You've just got the outsides of mouths."

"Well, how did it look to start with? When you first saw him? That's the question."

"There wasn't a first time. He was just there and his mouth was open right in my face." Her voice rose to a whimper. She drew back to her pillows and crouched there.

The fear, the terrible fear was back in her eyes.

John, bless him, kept sketching. Ignoring her. Letting the drawings of eyes, nose, long blond hair, sallow cheeks, ears, come together, waiting for her to forget herself and reach out once again to rescue his drawings. Head bent over his sketchbook, pencil scratching. A tug of wills. As one would deal with a child. Then she reached out a tentative hand. "Here. The ear. You need the ear. This is the one."

"Is it?" John asked without looking up. "We had two. Is that the one?"

Now she slid it to him. Firmly. "Yes. That's the one. That ear. Flat against his head, like a cat's." She leaned again toward the young man and his work. Drawing a picture. While Florence sat with her knitting. Careful now not to let the needles click. Two impostors, she thought, an old lady cop with gray hair and her knitting and a tough young man with his drawing pencil. And an old woman whose real wound was fear. That wound, Hendry thought, unlike the torn throat, might never heal.

John glanced her way, over the old head bent again now over his book. He had something at last!

The bastard! Hendry thought. That complete terrible sick bastard. Get him, John! Then we'll turn the galloping hordes loose street by street! And what? String him up to a lamppost?

Hendry, she said to herself, you are letting one vicious little criminal turn you into a lynch mob. She sighed. Her needles clicked comfortingly. She watched the two heads bent over the page and the swiftly moving pencil.

August 7

They sat over glasses of iced tea on a shaded patio, John's sketchbook propped in an empty chair with his box of pencils. They sat and listened to this rather handsome man, awkwardly perched on the edge of his chair.

"It's as if he knew what to do that would hurt her the most. She's always been proud of her breasts. She liked showing them off. You know, in good taste, pretty brassieres and low-neck blouses and dresses. Sometimes I think that's why she married a man with a dress shop." He laughed an uneasy laugh. "I'm not used to speaking in such personal terms. But it's hardly a usual time, is it? I'm not sure if I should call you Inspector or Mrs. Hendry. I'm not sure of the custom."

"I'm both, so either is nice." She smiled and waited for him to go on. Her knitting lay in her lap. It seemed to quiet people who were upset. He was that.

"I know she's watching from somewhere in there," Alistair said. He was tall, somewhere in his sixties. Trim, healthy-looking.

"We're not doing anatomical studies." John Carruthers drawled mildly, slouched in his chair. "Not of her, anyway. It's a damned awkward place to get bitten, I guess."

"She's used to being outgoing. It's been over three weeks and the bandage now is so small it doesn't show under a blouse. She dresses twice a day to go out, and for dinner. But she won't go anywhere. There's a neighbor just down the block who's a psychiatrist. I've talked to her. She advises that we just wait. It's better to let Carol decide to go out on her own, without undue prompting."

Florence Hendry was quiet, her eyes on her knitting. She let the needles click into the silence. John Carruthers sat comfortably, legs outstretched. Three quiet people, thought Hendry, each waiting for the other to speak. But they were practiced at it, she and John. Poor Mr. Alistair had no chance with them.

"It's not that she's particularly sexy," he said. "She's not that. She's a warm person but undemonstrative, I should say. She doesn't get all gushy about being a grandmother.

"She dresses to look nice, and likes to be taken out. Our only, well, intimate life seemed to be after the theater or the opera or dinner parties with interesting people. We'd get dressed up, leave the cars in the garage, call our favorite taxi driver." He laughed again; that deprecating laugh. "I confess we went out fairly often. Well . . ."

He got up and circled his chair, went to kick at a daisy bush, and came back restlessly to sit down again. "Well, it's a damned ugly place to get gouged by some madman's teeth. She remembers his teeth, she said, and his mouth. Like an animal. You'd think those nightmares would put a woman off sex altogether, but that hasn't been true. She's wanted comfort. We've slept in the same bed since she came home from the hospital. She's never done that in all our married life. We seem to make love all the time. It's just this living behind curtains. These weird spells she has. Not wanting to help with his picture. Not caring if he's arrested. She says she doesn't want to see his face anywhere, ever again. Ever. Then she breaks down altogether, does weird things. Here, let me show you." He got up abruptly, went into the house, returned holding a page torn from a magazine.

"Our daughter collected old movie magazines. Carol tore this one out, told me to give this to you when you came. Tell you this is the man she wants arrested."

He held out the page. John took it, looked puzzled, then handed it to her. "Means nothing to me."

Florence Hendry smiled. "You wouldn't know," she said. "It simply means that the Alistairs and I are of a similar age. It's an old photo of Tyrone Power, when he was young and dashing. The antithesis, I'm sure, of the blond-haired young man we're looking for. In fact"—she paused to look across to the older man—"it could almost be you at that age, couldn't it?"

Mr. Alistair smiled. "Yes. I looked something like that. I showed it to Dr. Phillips, our neighbor down the block, the psychiatrist. She just smiled and said, 'Enjoy. Live it up. Let's not do anything yet. Your wife has selected her own therapy.'"

"You know," Alistair said, "it's the first time in forty years of marriage that I've felt like a husband in the purely physical sense. Wanted. Needed. Even desired." He laughed again. "I rather like that part of it. I've stopped playing golf altogether. The stores just run themselves. The cook has been off visiting grandchildren. I do the cooking.

"It's this fear of going outside. She won't even come out here, where no one can see. She won't go through any door in the house that isn't standing open. The doctors have to leave their offices and come here to see her. When I suggest we go out, get some air, see our friends, she doesn't hear what I'm saying. She talks about something else. As if I hadn't said a word."

Florence Hendry watched him openly now. He wasn't aware of her gaze.

"Dr. Phillips, Leslie Phillips, our friend down the block, a good, bright woman. They're old friends. They play golf and tennis. Go to matinees. She's been here. She just smiles and says, 'Carol will walk out the door one day and come down to my house. Then we'll begin. She knows that. We've talked about it. First she's got to phone me, then walk down the street. She'll do it. You'll see.'

"But frankly, Mrs. Hendry, I don't see. I see a woman standing in front of the closed kitchen door I've forgotten to leave open sobbing because she can't just reach out and push it open. That's what I see, and I want my wife back. As she was." He smiled but his lips trembled and his handsome face was streaked with tears. "Warts and all."

The police car coasted down a slight grade, breasting the hot night air, windows open, moving through a canyon of squat warehouses interspersed with slim Victorian houses restored to an earlier elegance by darkness, bay windows staring blankly at the street. Roger had switched the radio to silence when they started down the block.

"About here, I think," Carrie said. "At the alley."

He touched the brake.

"Don't use the flood."

He let the car drift to the alley mouth and switched off the engine and the lights. They sat and listened, watching storefronts, some with dim night lights. Windows open to the night. No breeze to stir the curtains. Far down the block the blue light of a forgotten television glowed. Three blocks to the south tires thrummed on the hot concrete of the overhead freeway.

They waited in a silence broken only by the creaking of the car as it settled.

"I don't hear it now," she said.

They'd heard it a block away, just minutes ago, stopped by the blanketed form of a man on the sidewalk, naked feet sticking out obscenely beyond the end of a blanket cadged from the Salvation Army down the street. Shoes by his head. "He won't have those in the morning," Roger said. Waiting to see him breathe. Neither of them wanting to make the effort in this heat to get out and look, not wanting to wake him, either, just to make sure he was alive.

The blanket moved. The man stirred under it, coughed, and settled back again, his cheek on a concrete pillow.

It was then they heard the cry, at first directionless, filling the hot night air, a thin angry wail that was repeated with greater urgency or anger, perhaps pain.

"It's a cat," Roger said.

"No it isn't. I don't think it is. We'd better see."

The cries stopped abruptly. He drove to the end of the block and turned, switching off the chatter on the radio. Then the quiet squeaking ride down the block, listening.

She glanced at him. He waited, one hand on the wheel, no sense of urgency about him.

"I'll take a look down the alley," Carrie said. "It probably isn't anything."

Standing, she slid her stick into its sheath at her left hip, touched the mike button at her collar and heard the blast of air from her radio and from Roger's, then walked into the dark alley, leaving the broad street with its puddles of light. No suggestions of danger here, but she didn't walk down dark streets at night without him, as a rule.

Her leather belt creaked, heavy with gun and radio and can of Mace and cuffs. The stick banged gently at her leg. The alley was a deep, dark tunnel between elderly wooden houses three stories high. The streetlights here had long since gone out. The smells of a hundred years poured out the open windows with the heat. She walked, listening.

Around her, she knew, slept children whose cries beat against the traffic sounds in daylight in this alley, and bent old people who moved slowly out to shop, carrying string bags. Asians, most of them, today.

She walked between old cars that jammed the curbs on either side. She'd never heard it so quiet in the city. A black opening at her left hand. She stepped through into a courtyard bounded by the back sides of warehouses and apartments, clotheslines etched against the sky three stories overhead. Men's pants and shirts, dresses. No diapers. The windows around the yard were all dark.

The sound had been imperious, demanding, querulous. She'd heard the nighttime cries of her two nieces when they were very young. Perhaps like that, she wasn't sure.

She was about to turn away when she felt she was being watched, at her left shoulder. She pushed the thought aside but it persisted. She could feel the spot, and a scant moment later picked out, fifteen feet away on a low wood porch rail, the form of a big cat, staring at her. Then it opened its mouth and cried, a terrible rasping sound that ripped the silence of the courtyard and brought her adrenaline rushing. Her hand brushed the leather holster. The cat stopped on a last angry cry, closed its mouth and turned its head away, no longer bothering with Carrie.

"Damn!"

Her breath exploded in the single word, her heart pumped, hand flat on the leather. The cat, diminished in size, looking away, ignoring her, made her turn away in disgust so that her eyes looked directly into a dark window framed in summer curtains and right there, at eye level, saw two small girls in nightdresses with huge, luminous eyes, watching her. She could reach out and touch them. One said softly, "It's the cat. It woke us up."

Carrie found her eyes fixed to those big eyes and the soft forms in the window. "Do you think someone hasn't fed it?" The child's words were precise, touched with French. Vietnamese.

Carrie's hand went into her deep trouser pocket, found the wrapped hard candies there and brought them out. "I'm Carrie. Officer Carrie. Here. It's all right. It's candy."

Small hands reached out to pluck the candies one by one. The girls looked six or seven. She saw grave smiles.

"You'd better go to sleep," she said.

They nodded solemnly.

She reached out and touched a small hand, then turned away, moving back to the narrow gateway and the alley. It seemed bigger now. The black-and-white waited under the streetlight, Roger standing there.

He, too, regarded her with somber eyes.

"It was a cat," Carrie said.

Roger started up, flipping switches one by one. He let loose a sudden babble of urgent voices when he flicked on the radio.

"Mission Two, I'm going over to Second Avenue from California. There's no one on this street."

"Charley Four. I see you. You got a spot? Hit those bushes."

"This is Richmond One-oh-one. I'm in the unit block of Maple Street, going south. Do you have a description, Headquarters?"

The voice from headquarters droned, "Silence on the channel. Code thirty-three. Units, use pic channel three. Units, we have no description. This came in at 2333 hours. It is now 2352 hours."

Then the whispering radio silence.

"This channel will be used only for emergency transmissions," the female voice at headquarters said patiently. "All units not assigned, return to your districts. Repeat. Return to your districts."

Headquarters spoke with dogged patience when there

was too much excitement. "All units assigned to the area maintain silence on channel three except for emergency transmissions. For communications use pic channel three. Charley Four, return to the Potrero District. Mission Two, Mission Four, report to the One-oh-one in the Park District. Southern Three, Southern Five, proceed as directed into the Park. Report to the One-oh-one."

"We can't get pic three," Roger said. "Just on our pics. I don't think they'll work inside the car."

"Something's going on, with all that mess. Maybe we missed our call," Carrie said. "We'd better ask." She had the mike ready in her hand.

"We'd better wait," Roger said.

Headquarters came on again. "The Three Hundred is reporting to the scene. ETA five minutes. Richmond One-oh-one, request you return to the Richmond until your help is required. Other Richmond units previously detailed into the Park will remain in the Park."

The 101s were sergeants. The 300 was the night supervising captain.

Roger said, "It must be serious."

"Southern Four," headquarters droned.

"Southern Four," Carrie said. "We're clear."

"Southern Four, cover your adjoining sectors. Your three-car and your five-car have been sent to assist in the Park."

"Ten-four," Carrie said.

Roger started moving east toward the waterfront and the piers, empty at this time of night. Easy to watch from the car. He crisscrossed through the alleys as he liked to do. "Never let them know you're coming."

"I guess I blew it," Carrie said. "Chasing cats."

He didn't answer, took a corner slowly onto a main

street, working toward the three-car sector along the shipping piers.

"All channels," headquarters said. "We have a sexual assault on a child in the Park District. We have no description of a perpetrator. We have no car. Those units not specifically assigned to the Park will return to your districts, please."

Through the open windows, above the night traffic sounds, Roger and Carrie heard the thin urgent cry of the ambulance more than a mile away.

Headquarters again began intoning its mindless litany. "Units, traffic units have been assigned to clear major intersections from the Park to General Hospital. All units are cautioned to avoid the crime scene in the two hundred block of Locust. Units not assigned will return to their districts on order of the supervising captain."

In her mind, Carrie saw the neat row of homes and gardens along the 200 block of Locust Avenue where she once walked to her school, collecting milling groups of children along the way until they all arrived breathlessly together, a female Pied Piper and her band before the carved stone portals of the ancient school. The skin on her face was tight. The hot breeze through the window was cold against her cheek.

"That's my neighborhood!" she said with dismay. "That's where I taught school!"

They went about their business, coasting along Market Street, showing the black-and-white, a pair of alert stiff-backed police officers to the crowds of rollickers, as Roger called them, going from arcade to cheap clothing store to bar to another arcade.

Then the quiet back streets where shops had been shut down for hours now, checking the glass. If a shop door didn't reflect the car lights as they went by then someone had smashed it and some idiot burglar might be breathing inside, hoping they'd just drive by.

She banged on the door of a motor home parked by the canal. "Lock your doors and windows, please. You're in a No Parking zone but you can move it in the morning. Just lock it up." She heard somebody stumbling out of bed inside. The windows were pulled shut.

This wasn't Locust Avenue. No trees along these streets. No broad pavements with tree branches that swept down protectingly, so that residents had to prune them to let people walk along the sidewalks. Out there,

Carrie thought, the curbs were clear. People put their cars in the garage.

They pulled alongside a dust-covered family station wagon standing idle at a stoplight. The lights turned red then green then red again while a man and woman turned a street map this way and that, looking out the windows. Oregon license plates. Bundles of sleeping children in the back. "Lost in the big city," Roger said. They led them to a nearby motel with bright lights. "There's a pool," Carrie told the parents. "Don't let the children out on the street in the morning. It's not that kind of neighborhood."

"The price is right," Roger told them. "More like Oregon."

In the fourth hour of their night, headquarters intoned, "All channels. We have a report on the twelve-year-old girl from the Park District. She is considered critical and still unconscious. We have no report on her injuries. We have no description of a perpetrator. We have no car. It is requested that units use the land line to contact Southern Station, where the station keeper is in touch with the hospital."

Carrie used the floodlight to check the alleys. You could count the bricks. You could read the print on dirty newspapers shuffled along by puffs of hot wind.

She tried shifting on the seat, feeling sticky, rumpled, being strangled by pants designed for men, all crotch and no place for hips. It wasn't just the indignity, it was reality on hot nights on sticky plastic car seats. And her feet were wet in those damn shoes.

She glanced at Roger, his eyes moving quietly to right and left.

"Want to switch awhile? I'll drive it."

He shook his head no, and smiled.

She'd told her uncle, Spenser Lubick, "My partner's got an honest smile, and he doesn't go storming in and start a war. He just walks in big and honest as if he expects the war to stop. Sometimes it does."

But Roger's patience began showing signs of wear. Headquarters set them free for lunch. The other Southern cars were back from the Park.

"Empty-handed," Roger said.

She said, "I'll watch you eat a hamburger. I can't go swimming later with all that junk inside. I gave away my lunch."

"Candy lunch," he said.

A dirty black-and-white from the Potrero pulled in beside them at the drive-in. "You folks get to see the fun and games?"

"Not us," Roger said.

The other two were a pair, one black, one white, both big and untidy. "We already got us our quota," the white cop said. "We got two boys from the neighborhood thought they looked natural driving home in shiny new cars. Tootin' at the boys standing at the corner. Show their girlfriends." They both laughed.

"Our people don't drive cars," Roger said. "They take the bus. And we don't run around arresting them."

His comment silenced them. They turned away and went inside.

Carrie said, "Aren't we on the same side?"

"I'm not," Roger said.

In an age when crime victims were always underfoot, Roger said the next day as they waited for the lineup, from one to a dozen of them at any time of day or night snuffling around every district station in the city, suddenly every police officer on watch was so concerned with a single victim that quarters were dropping into pay phones all over town because cops had to know if the girl was still alive. Not even waiting until they got back to the station on relief to do it free, as they did their wives and girlfriends and drinking chums and soccer chums and creditors.

Which was meant, she supposed, to remind her she was not the only one. But it was neurotic to feel guilty about something that happened to a child halfway across the city.

The new lieutenant on the midnight watch in the Southern put on gold-rimmed reading glasses and laid his notes on the lectern to form up the watch. He gestured them into their chairs. He was tall and slim and his eyes smiled, or maybe that was just the glasses glinting. He wore old sergeant's stripes on neatly creased and faded blues.

"I'm Ian MacKenzie," he began, "posted acting lieutenant on this watch. I expect to stay in touch with the people at General Hospital. If there's a change in the child's condition, I'll put it out.

"Ten minutes ago, she was still unconscious with a head injury and bruises on her back. No weapon has been found. There are indications we're looking for a leather boot still on the perpetrator's foot.

"An inspector from the sex crimes detail is sitting at her bedside, probably with her knitting, looking like somebody's grandmother, which she is. She'll be there until the child wakes up. One of the parents is also at the bedside. They're taking turns.

"Now, on the perpetrator. That's thin. Residents were interviewed last night and the sex crimes people will be going through the neighborhood again today. So far, no one has seen a stranger on the street. The detail is unwilling for the moment to connect this incident with our series of sex crimes against old women in the Richmond and Park districts over the past three months. The uniformed patrols will make up their own minds about that." He smiled and took off his glasses to look out at them. "They always do, and sometimes they are right.

"There is a department composite on the bulletin board, and a description. I've never considered it dependable. Neither does the department artist who interviewed the victims, but it's all we've got."

"Otherwise it's business as usual. Sergeant McDowell will read out the night's orders." He stepped down and let McDowell take the roll call and read out crimes and criminals; then they all filed out into another hot night on the streets, the macadam soft and the concrete still hot from the sun.

Carrie and Roger parked on Sixth Street for their foot patrol from Sixth to Market, down to Seventh Street and past the Greyhound. Even the sidewalks were still hot.

Doors with the scratched and chipped remnants of names in gold or silver leaf marked the hotels whose rooms began up a flight of stairs, over the bars and pawn shops and crammed liquor stores and little markets, liquor bottles always at the front by the cash register, easily seen from passing patrol cars.

They timed their walk to begin when stores started shutting down, proprietors locking doors, money in their pockets as they walked nervously to cars in parking lots a block away. She and Roger locked the patrol car.

Doorways in the alleys were starting to fill up with sleeping forms. Above them, East Indian hotel managers waited for the Greyhound to bring them people who could buy a night in bed.

It was too hot to trudge up those stairs tonight to walk narrow hallways that still held the heat of day, to breathe in the smells. They stayed on the street. They watched the faces, some new, most of them old and dirty and familiar.

Carrie saw a man move furtively along the alley to bend over a sleeping form in a doorway. She tapped her stick against the brick wall of the building. The man glanced back at them and scurried on.

"You saved his wine," Roger said.

They walked through the cramped corner grocery, single file up one narrow aisle, past the cooler, down the other. The smells of the city were rich here, the odors of old cheese, spilled wine, the toilet gurgling in the store-room at the back.

The Pakistani grocer stood in the doorway as if waiting for a breeze. He said, "We have heard about the child. We are sorry."

His own children and his wife slept on the floor above, in rooms as cramped and hot as his grocery store.

Her training officer had once taken her into the Tenderloin just across Market Street, a block away, "to give you a smell of the real city," but she hadn't smelled the city until she'd started walking here with Roger on hot nights.

It wasn't like the Tenderloin. There, busy men and women, black and white, were always on the hustle. Still one minute, walking purposefully the next, looking busy. Women pausing to eye men in passing cars, turning to show breasts and buttocks, sometimes a pair of them chatting, laughing, but watching all the while to catch a passing eye. Then swinging about abruptly for no apparent reason to walk on, cross to the other side, back the other way, checking the shop windows as they walked to see who was watching from behind. Porno Row. Dirty bookstores, dirty movies, always busy.

Carrie tapped a wall again. Four idlers at an alley mouth shuffled and changed places.

Her winos and derelicts had no business down the street or anywhere. If they were sleeping, she looked after them. Awake, she shuffled them along.

She and Roger walked toward two white youths in dirty clothes eyeing the lighted shelves of bottles in the corner liquor store. They hadn't seen the uniforms.

She tapped her stick against the bricks.

The deep voice of Louise Alkron, her friend from Police Academy days, boomed over the radio when they started flipping switches and rolling down the windows in the radio car.

"Headquarters, we have a little traffic stop on Folsom, possibly a stolen car. No backup is needed. Oops! There he goes! Get him, George!"

Roger turned toward Alkron's sector and a moment later her voice broke in again. "Washoe's got him bottled up on Brush Street. He let the idiot escape down two dead-end streets!"

Then a moment later, quieter now, "All he can do in there is climb the walls, Headquarters. We're gonna sit right here and wait till he walks out."

Cheers and chortles on the radio, and the dry voice of headquarters summoning a backup, and MacKenzie.

The next call was for them. "Take the west side of a warehouse at Fourth and Brannan, Boy Four. Security heard sounds on the second floor. The dog unit will respond. Boy Three, take the east side, if you please."

Roger dropped her at a corner of the windowless four-story warehouse, at the alley, then drove to the far corner and got out. The fire escape was right in front of her. Handy for burglars to climb down. She saw the dog unit's station wagon pulling in at the end of the long block, Sergeant McDowell's car behind it. Both cars had their yellow flasher working, the eerie light flashing down the long alley. Just the thing to send some criminal clattering down her fire escape.

She touched the button at her collar and heard the whisper of static. Roger's voice said, "We'll let the dogs bite someone else this time. Maybe even the criminals."

She stepped back behind a steel light pole to get the flashing lights out of her eyes, recalling the dry voice of her training officer: "The person shooting at you could be a police officer. It often is."

She saw Roger at his corner, in his own puddle of streetlight, by his own light pole. Between them they could watch three sides of the building. She wished she'd left her hat on the car seat. She wished there was a breeze.

Some security guard was always calling for the dog unit, then remembering he might get bitten. Sometimes he was. He had to follow the dog unit through the building, floor by floor, but it was better than using half the watch walking up and down the aisles, climbing stacks of dusty crates looking for someone who could turn out to be a twelve-year-old boy.

Her radio whispered and she heard a man's voice. "We've got you in our sights now, Lubick. We're keeping an eye on the two of you." Then an obscene chortle.

God, she thought, and they let them carry guns.

It wasn't Washoe's frog-voice tones. She knew his

voice. George Washoe, transferred from the Central. When his name went up on the transfer list, Alkron said, "I know him. He brags he's been wearing the same uniform for six years. Jesus!"

When he was assigned to ride with her, Alkron was grim. "He's gonna have to buy another suit. We're gonna have an understanding!"

Washoe used to play with the radios. Now he had creases in his summer shirts. Anyway, he and Alkron were playing with a stolen car six blocks away.

The voice came again, "Roger Henderson, I wish *I* had a big good-looking girl to play policeman with."

Roger, being Roger, didn't answer. She watched him standing easily under his streetlight. She lifted her hat and wiped her sticky forehead and put it on again. The figures down the alley were becoming indistinct in graying light. Someone had turned the flashers off. Traffic was starting to move now, delivery wagons and early morning janitors, newspaper trucks, the drivers shoving stacks of papers into newspaper boxes at the corners. Quarter-eaters, Roger called them. "It always happens when the captain sends you out to get a paper. You can't just stand there in a police uniform and kick it open." All this before the lineup.

"Confiscate it," Washoe told him.

"I can't. They've got 'em chained."

Washoe said, "Call me over. I got bolt cutters in the trunk."

Ed Wellington chimed in. "That won't last long. Someone'll steal 'em."

Washoe looked out from under heavy brows and growled, "I got 'em chained."

Headquarters gave them a code four. Go back on patrol. No burglars in the building. Maybe just a wobbly box fell off the stack. Maybe mice. She and Roger heard the early morning traffic stops, calls for tow trucks to clear strange cars out of driveways so citizens could drive to work. The silent alarms were coming in, heard at security firms and relayed to police. Like clockwork, every day at seven A.M. when sleepy store managers opened businesses and forgot to switch off the alarms. "Must be broken," they told police. Roger said, "We have noticed there is a high failure rate at seven A.M." Once, he said, he found a burglar. Everybody was surprised.

At eight-thirty, as they turned back for the station, knots of children began marching across intersections, halting the commuter traffic. They circled one another, danced and dawdled, but they moved as if held together by a magnet. She saw two young girls in summer frocks, long black hair down their backs. She couldn't see their faces. Were those her nighttime friends?

When they got in, Washoe sat at the long table writing his report. An officer she didn't know sat beside him. He had a blue streak on his tongue where he'd been sucking at his ballpoint pen. He qualified for the idiot on the radio. Once she was sure, they'd have a talk.

MacKenzie stood there patiently, waiting to read and sign reports. He had smile lines around his mouth and eyes. An outdoor face.

By the time she'd changed, Roger had already gone, out to the high school track for his morning run. Alkron caught up with her and said, with a nod in the direction of the acting lieutenant, "He is Sergeant Ian MacKenzie, transferred out of Sex Crimes, soon to be posted as lieutenant, and not long after that, no doubt, named on the captain's list. He's a comer. That mean anything to you?"

"Not to me," Carrie said.

"I got a friend up there," Alkron said. Alkron had friends everywhere, mostly men. "He's been working the rape cases. They say he volunteered to go back in uniform because he's sure the rapist is right here in the Southern. That's a dumb reason for giving up a nine-to-five job with weekends off but otherwise he's pure gold. He's got friends in high places. He isn't even married."

Carrie said, "His uniform fits. I noticed."

Alkron said, "My partner is investing in new blues. I pointed out the cleaners, so he knows where it is. He just needed guidance."

When they passed the bulletin board, Carrie saw a note in a large, neat hand. "She's holding her own and the doctors say they're optimistic." Signed "MacKenzie."

"I've got four days not to think about it," she told Alkron.

It would take her an hour to wind down. She'd do laps at the high school pool, then put on real clothes for her drive into the country. She'd be herself again, not this fat-feeling untidy person who walked around in baggy pants wearing thirty pounds of gun and gear.

It was hot. Walking through the lot, she squinted against the brightness and found the drawing of the rapist was still with her, etched somewhere behind her eyes, that young man with stringy hair down to his shoulders and a thin, pinched mouth, and insane eyes.

She took her blues out onto the small back porch to brush them before hanging them away. The belt and holster of plain black leather, still stiff with newness, she laid out along a bottom shelf at the back of her closet, behind her clothes and shoes, and lowered the lid and heard it click shut and lock. The closet locked, too. Any good burglar could open it, but kids in the neighborhood would have a hard time. Her friend Bullard told her, "If they see a row of uniforms with patches and don't know by then they're in a cop's house, then they're too dumb to find the gun. But I would be embarrassed to have some kid shoot up the neighborhood with my revolver."

So she had a shelf built and locked it away. Bullard, with his big belly and rambling philosophies, was part of the mosaic of her one year and a few months as a police officer. He'd been an older partner and a friend in her training days in the Northern.

Bullard was shot once by a kid in the neighborhood, one of a gang of kids in a doughnut shop with his gun on the proprietor. Bullard said, "I walk inside and see him.

I couldn't shoot. The place is full of kids and people. I said, 'All right, asshole, put it on the floor.' Instead he pulled the trigger, hit me in the leg. He said, ·'I paid twenty dollars to rent it. I want to see if I got cheated.' I tell him, 'Ask 'em at San Quentin. You just bought a ticket.' By then my partner gets his ass inside and cuffs him. ·

"My wife comes to the hospital and tells me I made the whole thing up. She thought I shot myself. She was surprised I got a commendation."

Bullard laughed. He had a real laugh. And he smoked cigars. Carrie didn't like men who smoked cigars, but she liked Bullard.

He had run in on one of the rapes a month ago. One of the older women. Walking her tiny dog at midnight in her own neighborhood. She went out and left her door wide open, the light spilling out on the lawn and flowers, and the guy pulled her back inside her own house and shut the door. That's what a neighbor noticed. The door was shut and the dog was outside yapping. She never left the dog outside. Bullard said, "This is a bad man. He picks the frail ones. They don't even have a good scream."

Carrie only saw him now when he brought a prisoner down. Or came for the mail. They sent Bullard on the duty runs and knew he'd come back without stopping for a horn. He just wanted his cigar. He treated himself to one a day.

She was daydreaming, she told herself. But she'd straightened up the small apartment, packed her bag, picked up the mail. A letter from her sister in New Hampshire, where her husband taught in a prep school. Carrie didn't open it. Her uncle would want to read it with her. The books she was reading—a history of California towns and a mystery. Then she was out and in her car and driving over the Golden Gate Bridge. She drove toward the even warmer weather of the town of Forestville, beyond the golden hills, tucked in among neat lanes of apple trees, where her friend and uncle, Spenser Lubick, raised his roses and green beans and basil and lemons, and hung out his shingle, mostly hidden in a privet hedge: S. LUBICK, CPA.

"When I have that sign made," he'd told her long ago, "I'll have them put 'RET.' on it so my neighbors know I don't have to work. I intend to be selective."

"Choosy," she'd corrected him.

When he'd finally done it, left all his city work behind and traded the tall house above the bay for a country bungalow, she'd challenged him about the sign. "Why don't you? Like some old general?"

"It was a private joke. Money is a basic drive. Like squirrels hoarding nuts for winter. People don't want the family doctor making jokes about their sex lives, either. They just want to know it's going to be all right."

"We all want that."

"Some more than others. You never seemed to need much reassurance, or correcting, either."

"But I have you, Spenser," and she'd laughed. It was true, she'd had him growing up, uncle, friend and crusty adviser.

He'd told her once when she was still a schoolgirl and they'd gone fishing in the surf, "We're cut from the same tree, Carrie. You read my mind better than your aunt does."

Another time, when her aunt had died, he said, "It isn't the sex I miss so much, or the warm body in the bed, though I miss those more than I thought I would, but being myself alongside another human being."

Now she was thirty-two and they called her Lubick in the city, and he was her only family, with her parents dead and her sister in the East driving a timid husband into spurts of professional activity.

Spenser said, "Your sister's found someone who's flattered that she'd bother. Now she'll leave us alone."

Carrie missed her sister, those annoying, prying, demanding phone calls every day. Whom did she phone now?

She felt cool in her light clothes and pretty shoes, driving, her mind rambling.

She hadn't told Spenser until she had the letter giving her a date to start at the Police Academy. Then they'd gone out to sit at the cliff's edge above the ocean. She told him about looking through her closets at all those dresses and smart suits and rows of shoes.

And faced for the first time that she was trading those for blue pants and a jacket with a gold patch at the shoulder.

After her first week she'd written him, "I can't stick the shoes. They weigh ten pounds. If I quit, you'll know why. I refuse to walk around forever in lead weights disguised with shoelaces."

She wrote him about her trip to the uniform shop and the salesman who wanted her to buy an Italian leather holster with a spring clip for an easy draw. He thought she was shopping for her boyfriend.

The shop was full of men who towered over her. She said more loudly than she meant, "That's not my style. I'm shopping for myself."

She wrote him, "They all turned away and the helpful

smiles disappeared. They put on their blank cop faces. When I was a pretty schoolteacher, they came to show off to the children in the schoolroom just to make a date."

She'd laughed and shed tears when she laid out her new things for Spenser and they agreed her petite sister would drawl, "They're nice, Carrie, but they're not very feminine."

But at the last it came down to the shoes. She could bear it if everyone thought her bottom was really shaped like this, but those shoes!

Spenser let her storm and protest, then he said, "You're as full of quirks as she was. You get what you want and then you've got to find something wrong with it."

Her aunt was the "she" in Spenser's conversation. That slim and beautiful woman. By simple reference he kept her near, as if she were in some other room just out of sight.

"It's a trait of femininity, I guess," he said.

"And men are full of strength and stoicism."

"You've got it."

"And you sound like a cop," she said. "You've been practicing."

She had to laugh. Dear Spenser. He wrapped wise counsel in bright packages to make her smile.

She drove past her usual turnoff through the farmlands and stayed on the freeway into Santa Rosa, to the butcher shop for thinly sliced veal for scallopini, and fresh eggs, then to the next-door market for the espresso coffee they both liked. The tennis shop to pick up her newly strung tennis racquet.

Then on her way again into the rolling hills with their

dairy herds and green oak trees, and down into the small flat farms with neat rows of apple trees. All these people she had known, whose children she had taught in her first classes in a country schoolroom. Hard-working people guided by strict rules laid down by the seasons. Something like police officers.

Spenser would have seen the newspaper stories about the rape of the child. She wouldn't have to tell him about that, she thought grimly. He'd have read all the papers, as he'd read the stories of the earlier crimes. The newspapers would be stacked neatly in a cupboard, waiting to wrap fruit and vegetables to give away to city friends, and to start fires in winter. Not because the crimes were suddenly her job. Because it was his world.

There'd be time for a nap in her big-windowed room in the low farmhouse, touched with the night's coolness and fresh with the scent of lemon trees outside her windows. She was tired, but the long night was gone, the ten long nights of her week were behind her somewhere with the stark drawing on the wall. And the children, eyes big and luminous, small hands touching hers in the darkness. Oh, those children! She'd tell Spenser about that!

She saw the stained brown shingles and the two brick chimneys above the privet hedge and turned down the lane to pull up abruptly next to John La Pointe, waiting for her, ten years old and self-appointed watchman of the four houses on the half mile of country lane. Legs too long for his patched pants and skinny with the burning energy of good health. He was chatting at her before the car came to a stop.

"I was listening for the car. I can tell it by the sound. Did you know that? I can tell it's four cylinders by the whine and it's got a funny squeak in back when you take the curve. I wanted to tell you I traded that old baseball bat for a skateboard. It needs new wheels. If you take me into Santa Rosa with you next time I know where to get some. I'm going to paint it black and green, with a dragon!"

Nonstop. She thought of the sweeping grades of the blacktop highway where cars and trucks traveled sixty miles an hour, and sighed. At least she wouldn't have to watch. She found herself saying, "Okay, but no highways on the weekends."

"Okay." Cheerfully.

She pulled in under the acacia tree in the gravel patch for her car, bordering the lawn. Spenser kept his shiny car in the small barn.

"Did you arrest anybody last night?"

"Not last night. But I saw a man go through a Stop sign."

"Did he get a ticket?"

"No. He didn't mean to do it."

John found that boring. "Your uncle said he had a paying client and he'll be back this afternoon."

Paying, indeed. Spenser's fees were small but his satisfaction plentiful.

John carried in her packages while she collected books and bag.

"How's your mother?" she asked.

"She's all right, but my brother causes her a lot of grief. They're a lot of trouble when they're five."

"I guess you were, if I remember."

"Yeah." He grinned.

"I'm going to have a nap. Tell your mother I'll come by later on."

"Okay. She said she's got tomatoes and some cucumbers. You can have all of those." He made a face.

"When I wake up," she said. "Tell her."

"Okay." The screen door slammed on the sound of his voice. She liked that ringing bang. It meant you were home, shut inside this cool house with the Gravenstein apple branches spreading overhead.

Her bed with its white coverlet. A breeze touched the

white curtains. Jennie's letter waited still unread on the hall table. She stripped and lay back and closed her eyes. The bang of the screen door rang in her head. So frail a sound to keep out the whole world. She slept.

She woke to the searing smell of cordite and the jarring explosions, the blast of heat past her cheek, the weight of her .38 revolver heavy in her hands one moment, pulling her arms skyward the next as she squeezed off round after round in even tempo. It was the heat, the sun full in her windows, the curtains flat. She was perspiring.

The roar of the dreamed explosions faded in the silent house. She heard her uncle's voice on the telephone. That was reality, that crisp voice.

She showered and pulled on a summer dress and sandals, pulled a brush through her hair. It was hot. She found him working at the kitchen table.

"That was Nellie, our favorite waitress. She thinks Uncle Sam is charging her too much for tips she's too old and ugly to get anymore. I explained that when she was young and beautiful she didn't pay enough. That took her mind off taxes.

"By tomorrow she'll remember she was never young and beautiful and she'll phone again. I can't tell her life cheated her, not the government."

"Doesn't she have a point, though?"

Spenser said, "She was born with umbrage. That didn't make her beautiful. She's beautiful when she's carrying plates of food to hungry customers. And graceful as a ballet dancer. Which brings us to that package in the icebox, from the butcher."

"Dinner," Carrie said. "One of your favorites."

"Anything's my favorite when I can take my evening stroll and come back to find it on the table. Then I'm a country squire."

She said, "I'm going over to see Rosalee and collect tomatoes and things. I was counting on green beans. Shall I pick some lemons to take over?"

"All in the cooler. Lemons and green beans. I like the barter system. I don't have to itch tending tomato plants. I'm just glad God doesn't make me cut and carry firewood in this heat. I can enjoy that when it's cold."

That was Spenser. God and the barter system were on his side, and the government could be handled.

He had torn out the inside walls of this house when they'd bought it and made a big kitchen and a pantry on the cool side in the afternoons, with morning sun in the broad windows. A long ship's table served as his desk in the daytime, a dining table at night, his typewriter and calculator put away, papers and reference books in cupboards. He was tidy.

The other rooms held the culled favorites of the antiques and Persian rugs from their two houses, and the paintings, prints and etchings already owned or collected in their travels. Spenser liked to wander from one small hotel to another through England and Scotland, with his fishing gear. She liked the churches and museums of the Continent. They both liked old books and old things.

"I see your new chief on television in his gold braid, with the mayor. He looks impressive. There was a story on the rape of the little girl. Is she going to be all right?"

"They don't know yet. It doesn't have much to do with me. That's for the experts in the bureaus."

He got up to pour iced tea from the refrigerator. He was lean and supple, white-haired and tanned. A beautiful figure of a man, within three years of seventy. Hands slim and brown with pruning in his garden and doing chores about the house that he might have hired done. He could hire someone to breathe for him, too, he said, or to listen to music. His eyes were gray, like MacKenzie's.

"We have a new sergeant as acting lieutenant, transferred from the sex crimes detail back into uniform. There are rumors he's after the rapist."

"So he's working in disguise."

She hadn't thought of that. She laughed.

"Oh, Spenser."

He said, "I've cleared tomorrow morning. All those demanding clients. I thought we'd drive over to the club and you can try out the new tennis pro. I asked him to set aside some time from all the teenage girls and housewives who find tennis slimming. You can find out if he likes tennis."

"Good. I've got to work the city out of me."

He understood. He knew the city. He wasn't on the boards of corporations now. Only rarely did he get dressed up in city clothes to go in and have lunch with old friends. He told her, "I'm not camping out. I live here." He worked with the local church, the schools. He was on the water board, finding money to build dams to hold the winter rain, contending with the city people for water the farmers needed. He went up to the legislature in his khakis, not a charcoal suit.

Out the window she could see the small barn tucked into the beginning rows of apple trees. Beyond, the low round hill, bright in the sun, was studded with uplifting crags of serpentine. The cows had gone to shade on the other side.

"All right." She got up briskly. "I'll call the pro, then go see Rosalee."

She walked in the shade of elm trees that rose sixty feet over the lane and cast long shadows in late afternoon, planted by the same man who'd built the carved Victorian farmhouse Rosalee and Anton owned at the end of the lane. Even the two newer homes had been here fifty years, hidden down long curving driveways in the apple trees.

In the city, when you blinked, something changed. Like that night at the traffic barricade when she'd asked her relief, one of the old cops, "What were those buildings they just knocked down?" and his face went blank.

She laughed at him. "I can't remember either."

"Warehouses," he said firmly.

"No they weren't. There was a radio shop on the corner, then a bar. What else?"

He said brusquely, "Get a fireman."

He got on the radio, calling the sergeant. "Costain, get down here to Fourth and Howard!" Then there were three of them holding their hats and scratching their heads and laughing at one another.

Or, there was, if just briefly, before a squat concrete block warehouse filled the empty space, a tall spindled Victorian, its peaks five stories high. One wet night she watched as that graceful building with its intricate woodwork went up in roaring flames amid the useless arcs of a dozen fire hoses, and an old fireman with a wet, sooty face, taking a breather, told her that seventy years ago laughing girls had come running down those curving back stairs in pretty frocks to greet young sailors just up from the docks. "The grandest whorehouse in the whole city!" he said proudly. Only the street signs remained, Annie and Alice and Minna and Clementina, the narrow alleys of the Southern.

But here nothing had changed for a hundred years.

She walked between white wooden gates and over cool grass to the white-painted porch with etched glass over the door and the coolness of polished floors through the screen.

Rosalee, a slim, vigorous woman with blond hair swept back, a narrow alert face and starched apron, pushed open the screen door.

She told Spenser after dinner, "I'm glad the cheese factory is flourishing. Four more housewives from the neighborhood working for him and a contract with a market chain for brie and breakfast cheese. Is that success at last?"

"Anton is a prudent man. He waited long enough to make the leap. Now his children will go to the best schools and he'll have money in the bank, and never sell a bad wheel of cheese."

He dealt the cards. This was their ritual, begun in the city house at this same baize table after her parents died and Spenser's house became the home she came to on school holidays. He'd check up on her while her aunt made disapproving sounds from her reading chair.

"Where's that boyfriend with the golden curls?" he'd said.

"Spenser, really." Her aunt, from her chair.

"Oh, I don't mind," Carrie had said. "He looks like a Greek god but he won't make the Olympics."

"I don't care about his plans," Spenser had said. "I wanted to know yours. He used to be underfoot on weekends."

"A summer idyl. We had youth and beauty, and we swam together, then I grew up and he found someone else to be his towel girl. I think he married her."

Years later, two degrees and several boyfriends later, one night with her aunt's chair empty, no longer pulled out to the fireplace with her reading lamp and sewing table, he'd said, "Carrie, I don't want this big house anymore. Maybe it's time to start new memories. I've had my eye on a small place in the country. I wondered if you'd like to share it."

She'd said, "I can't go off and lick the world if you and I don't have a home somewhere."

"Good!" Spenser said. "I was afraid we'd have to get all sentimental. Tomorrow we'll drive up and look at it. No view of the bay, no swimming pool or tennis courts. Just trees. Rows of apple trees. I don't know why they appeal to me. They just do."

She'd said, "We don't need fifteen rooms. We can probably make do."

They'd walked through Forestville, a town with one street and two gas stations and a general store, doctor's office, restaurant, bar and the inevitable antique shop. In time she knew it as a place where she seldom met a stranger.

They'd spent an entire summer rambling together through Europe and England and Scotland while workmen repaired and painted the small house and barn.

Many canasta games ago.

A cool breeze came in the open windows. Crickets were starting.

"I'm glad your sister's comfortable," he said. "Even if she isn't sure she likes what you're doing, she isn't here to watch, and I don't have to listen to it."

"Standing around all night outside a warehouse isn't likely to upset her."

"I suppose. Except you could get shot."

Spenser glanced up at her and slowly spread his cards out on the table.

She was exasperated, left holding a full hand. "I never learn. You get my mind on other things and never let yours wander. You're always doing that!"

He noted the scores carefully in his neat script, then shuffled and began dealing again. "I liked your letters about Roger. He seems to get better as you go along."

She said, "The more I learn, the smarter he gets. He lets me rattle around while he does his thing, just watching everything. We're all work talk. No sex talk, not even about his love life. He cooks and cleans and visits his parents up in Washington State, and writes his brothers and sisters, and does his job.

"And he runs," Carrie went on. "I didn't tell you that. We bumped into one another going through the gate at the high school when I was going for my swim. But he doesn't fish. I asked him."

"Fishing?" Spenser asked.

"I think I'll have to marry a fisherman," she said soberly. "They talk to their children, like you talked to me. All those times we were wrestling fishing poles and perch. You said things you'd thought about a lot, and I thought about them, too."

"There's not much I can say about what you're doing now," he said.

"That's all right. I have Bullard. He's my graduate course in being a policeman, but I think he'd be flustered to know he's become my mentor. I've got two stories, though, I haven't told you yet. Want to hear them?"

"If you can play and talk and not make excuses afterward," Spenser said.

"We'll walk, instead. I'd like the air."

They put the cards away. She put on walking shoes. They stepped out into a dark tunnel under the tall elms along their country road.

She said, "You know, I don't think he's got a heart of gold. But he's no bully, just big and blunt. That's how he came across to me the first time I met him.

"It was one of my last weeks with the training officer. Still early in the midnight watch. We heard this commotion on the air and a call for backup. We started over. Then the call for a wagon. Someone making a handful of arrests. We found a crowd spilled out of a bar, carrying their glasses with them, and two officers with their faces and uniforms all messed up wrestling the handcuffs on two guys. Hats and sticks were scattered in the street. All four of them were bloody.

"We helped them herd their prisoners into the back seat and picked up their gear. One had his radio smashed. Then the crowd started moving back and I noticed this fat cop sort of waving them along. He wasn't even saying anything. He wasn't looking all that mean, just business-like, but they were moving. They all went back inside the bar.

"Then I saw he had two men standing by themselves, looking foolish. They just stood there while he cuffed them together. We said we'd take them in. I knew he was the foot beat along there. But he said, 'No. Nothing serious here. A little public intoxication. We'll just walk on in. It'll clear our heads.' And he did. Ten blocks.

"I could see him lighting his cigar, his prisoners waiting until he got it lit, then starting off again. And these two cops were straightening their clothes and wiping the blood off their faces. Their prisoners looked a mess in the back seat. Talking about felony charges for assault on a police officer.

"They could see Bullard walking along, way down the street, and one had the gall to say, 'Maybe he'll buy 'em an ice cream cone.'

"When we pulled away my training officer said, 'That's Bullard. He keeps the peace.'

"Later, I walked with him a few nights. I learned the names of all the merchants on the street. When they closed. When their wives were expecting babies. And the strangers, too. Where they lived. The cars they drove. How many days they'd been around. He saw everyone. We straightened out some messes, little ones. He said I had the knack. Whatever that is.

"He taught by parable, too, but I bet he'd laugh to hear me say it. He used to walk a beat in the Southern, my sector along Sixth Street, on the swing watch, late afternoon. He'd been there six months. He wasn't anybody's best friend. He played it straight. They got to know him.

"Once he was walking down the block and somebody whispered from a hotel door, 'Watch the redhead. He's got a knife.' By that time he'd gone by but he didn't turn. He kept on. He shook out the loungers in the doorways. Then heard it again. 'He's got a knife! He's going to get a cop!'

"He moved along. He didn't turn but he used the store windows to look behind his back. People weren't looking at him. But he heard another whispered warning before he got to the corner. It was clear. The crowd had moved away, left space all around him. He stood watching reflections in the window of the news vendor's shack, standing with his stick in both hands. He saw the hotel door behind him open, a flash of red hair, and he turned in time for a full swing at the man's face, clubbed the knife away and helped him down with a knee in his back, and had him cuffed on the ground while one of the street people used the corner phone, calling nine-one-one."

They walked with strides well matched. The dark road ended at the drive to the La Pointe farm, and the family dog came out to sniff their hands.

Spenser said, "Does that tell you something about violence you didn't know?"

"No. I know about violence. The playground's not much different. Except for the knife. At school they'd say, 'It's God's own mess out there today. Send Miss Lubick,' and I didn't mind. I seemed to handle it.

"What Bullard said was they'll help you if they can. If you're straight. They don't want you getting hurt. But they're not the cop. You are."

Spenser said, "All right, I've got Bullard's moral. Now what's yours?"

"Everybody's pulling strings to get into the bureaus. I don't want to get ahead that way. I want to work on the street. I can make sergeant there. That's where I want to be."

"I won't argue," Spenser said. "You didn't want to be a towel girl, either."

They walked awhile, then Spenser said, "How big was that knife, by the way?"

Carrie laughed, and the sound, a soprano bell, lifted into the dark umbrella of the trees. "It's as big as Bullard wants to make it. Listen." She took his arm. "You've got to picture the cigar ash dribbling down my uniform."

She deepened her voice and used her hands. " 'I shove this sucker in the wagon and I look around for that pig-sticker and it's gone. While I'm cuffin' the asshole, someone sneaked up and stole it!' "

She took off her shoes to walk through the cooling grass to the front door. The luminescence of the night touched the roof of the small barn and the half mile of treetops that dipped down to the small creek that marked their land.

Spenser said, "We'll take John with us to the club. He'd like to play some tennis."

She said, "We could even go to church on Sunday. I'd like that. We could stop by the river after and not have to cook."

He said, "You haven't talked much about your new Sergeant MacKenzie."

"Oh," she began, stretching her arms up toward tree limbs and the sky, "I guess there isn't much to say. He's as tall as you, or taller, and his hair is going gray, and he has a kind of beauty."

She heard her words and thought, Well, that's true, enthralled with the coolness and the way her body felt, loose and long, reaching upward. The summer Gravensteins were starting to fall now. Soon the autumn apples would be ripening in the rows of trees down to the little river.

She'd get up early and make bread and apple pies. She lay between cool sheets and her mind filled with white flour sifting down on the board. She thought, I'll make three pies.

Her eyes opened before the first ring ended. She saw it was eleven o'clock as her hand picked up the phone. Saturday night. She was oriented now. "This is the station keeper on the swing watch. We've got a fire at Eleventh and Natoma, the block with the bathhouses, four alarms going to five. I'm to call in all the watch off weekends. Those I can find."

She was standing, holding the phone and pulling clothes out of drawers.

"I can smell the damn thing from here. The halls are filling up with smoke. It looks like the Mission District firebug has moved into the Southern."

Chatty. Almost cheerful about it.

"You are to pick up Sergeant MacKenzie at his home and bring him in. He's got no wheels. I got no car to send."

She said, "On my way," and hung up.

She pulled on slacks and shirt and shoes and picked up a sweater and her purse. Spenser stood sleepily at his bedroom door.

"Want some coffee to wake up?"

"I'm awake. We had enough at dinner. I've got a fire going near my sector, the next one over. A lot of kids and old people and old buildings. See you Wednesday in two weeks. I hope we can fish and go to church."

She drove south, angling toward the freeway, driving swiftly on the deserted country roads. She made good time but watched for dawdlers. The bars were still open, the drunks still on their barstools, most of them.

The freeway lanes from the city were bright with headlights even this late at night, people escaping the hot sidewalks. Not many cars going in her direction.

In her apartment the air was hot. Her pants and shirt were heavy after three days of freedom. The gunbelt and revolver were always lead weights when she first strapped them on. Her stick and radio were in her locker. Her hat was in the hall closet. She was ready.

MacKenzie was at the curb, on a street that curved off the flat avenues and up a wooded hill she hadn't even known was there, in the city. His uniform was neatly pressed but old and almost gray under the streetlight. He slid in.

"Thanks," he said. He put his hat on the seat between them. "The truth is, I don't like hats."

He was big enough. He just wasn't threatening. Alkron said he never had trouble with a prisoner. She thought, They just walk in quietly? Like they do with Bullard? Then turned to her driving.

He said, "I left my car in Santa Rosa. My daughter is about to have a baby and they need a second car, just in case."

She said, "That's where I spend my weekends. With my uncle."

He smiled at her. "I got a ride to the bus. Thought I'd save you a few miles."

They dropped down into the city and she saw the clouds of smoke rolling upward, hiding the city lights, making a black hole in the sky over the Southern. "We're probably the last ones in," he said. "We'll ride together and see what's needed."

The station keeper said, "It's contained. That just came over. The whole city didn't burn but I guess you're needed anyway. It burned three hours and a half and took out half a city block. The captain's there. The coroner came in himself so I guess they have some fatals. It's the firebug, all right. I knew he'd kill someone, sooner or later."

They collected radios and put in batteries.

On the street the smoke rolled overhead. A breeze lifted it out of the small canyons of the alleys but it clung to the broad streets. MacKenzie left her with a begrimed officer of the early watch at a traffic barricade. She touched the button at her collar, heard the blast. She was downwind tonight. It was her turn to stand in the smoke.

The other officer said, "I heard about one body, an old lady or a child, they don't know which."

Firemen walked from the alley with blackened hands and faces, yellow oxygen tanks on their backs, masks pushed aside, their heads dripping water. An early crew. They'd been back through the buildings, room by room, to make sure.

She heard Alkron's voice in a blast of air. "Watch those guys in front of the bar in the middle of the block. They want to be firemen."

She saw the bar with the knot of men outside and walked toward it, but she couldn't see Alkron through the smoke in the long block stacked with ladder trucks and fire engines and the crisscross of white hoses against wet pavement. Arcs of gray water rose over the tops of the four-story warehouses and disappeared into the roiling mess of smoke and occasional tongues of flame. Fire was still burning somewhere in the middle of all that, inside the block where people lived alongside warehouses.

She shifted her belt and pulled her pants straight. Baggy but warm. She didn't feel grimy yet but she would. She paced between the bar and the corner, watched streams of water rise out of the midblock smoke and arc back into smoke. Her eyes began to burn and she kept her mouth closed against the stench of old wood and old clothes burning. She kept waving cars away. People wanted to watch from the comfort of their cars, windows rolled up tight, parked in the middle of the street.

"Under-control time was five minutes ago," she heard Alkron say.

The next time she looked she could see all the way down the street. Two ambulances, a Red Cross bus, police officers at the barricade, a knot of firemen, one white hat among the black hats. The fire chief fought a fire from upwind, out of the smoke, not down here.

More firemen were leaving now, going back to quarters. There were clusters of people in nightclothes and blankets at the far end of the block, one group of young men in white robes and towels. Bathhouse customers. Like those who, in an earlier fire, had died in their cubicles, some of them. She could see children wrapped in blankets inside the lighted Red Cross bus.

A radio car stopped to pick up the other officer. She hadn't even learned his name. She waved the cars along. She heard the captain on the air, returning to the station.

He'd go home for breakfast. He probably wasn't even dirty.

Soon the salvage crews would move in and start unlacing layers of fire hose.

She saw MacKenzie walking from the mouth of the alley, his hands and his face like the firemen's, sleeves and shoulders gray with ash and black with soot. He'd been in the fire.

"Just one person died," he said. "A four-year-old girl. She ran into a closet."

Was he the one who found her? Anyway, he'd gone to see. He looked grim.

She asked, "Was it the arsonist? We haven't had him here before."

"No. It wasn't arson. It started in a kitchen and ran up the curtains into a light well. This old wood is always ready to burn. We lost two apartment houses. They'll have to be torn down. A clothing warehouse with a lot of cottons ready for shipping. That will smolder for a while. One bathhouse. Fifty people will need some place to live."

"At least it's not the firebug," she said.

"Not yet," he said. "We'll regroup in about an hour, I think. I'll send a car to relieve you. Keep this street closed off. They'll need to keep working here. I'm going to the station for dry clothes."

She said formally, "All right, Sergeant," and he looked blankly at her, then he smiled. "To tell the truth, I never have liked fires. I didn't thank you for the ride."

She said, "I drive every day until you get your car back."

He slapped at his shirt and pants, then slid into the

radio car. "I'll say yes, and thanks, until I get some other form of transport."

The sky was turning from the color of dirty smoke back into blackness. She could see the skyscrapers in the business district. She thought, We send all our smoke to Oakland.

The flashing red lights were turned off now. The hoses were flat against the street. She heard pumps in the alley and water began rushing along the curb. They were pumping out the basements.

A radio car pulled up to the barricade with Bill Whitaker driving. She knew him from her training days. "Leave it while I check the alley," Carrie told him. "Then you better park it or some clown will hit it."

He was still clean. He grinned at her. "They're sending the three-car to take over. We're going back on patrol, you and I. They couldn't find your partner.

"Anyway, I'm glad you know the territory. I've been in the Richmond. All I know is hippies and art museums."

She drove—they were her streets—and Whitaker talked about the rapes.

"It was always on our watch. We had the first two in the Richmond, then he moved this way, into the Park and Northern. He picks women in their sixties, you know, old types who can't sleep, so they take their exercise at midnight. Anyway, they used to.

"We always got the calls when we were coming on the street. He was doing it while we were standing there at lineup and the old watch was jockeying to get off. Then this time he caught that little girl and her dog."

Carrie said, "The dog wasn't in the teletypes."

"Then they're saving it for nut confessors. He kicked it to death. A little gray terrier. They found it in the gutter."

Carrie shuddered. She couldn't face a small dead dog.

Whitaker said, "It wasn't even a priority call. Some neighbor called in a disturbance, said she heard someone shouting to leave her dog alone. She didn't even say it was a child. They got there and found her moaning in the bushes.

"He kicked the little girl, too, before or after. She wasn't five feet tall."

The picture was too real. She pushed it away and turned her eyes back to the streets.

They made a circuit of the sector, then drove back and stopped at the alley where firemen were shoveling out the muck, and with it children's dolls and framed photographs and table lamps. Some things not even smashed but nothing that wasn't black and dripping.

Another radio car stood sentry at the far end of the alley, checking people who wanted to walk down, the ones who didn't look as if they lived there, who weren't Spanish or Vietnamese or twenty-year-olds with old faces wearing castoff clothes. Morning came gray.

At the station she learned that MacKenzie had sent Washoe and Alkron home. They were the first ones to barge into the burning apartment house and bang on doors and haul people out, then run shouting through the bathhouse. No one was talking about who opened the closet door. Possibly a fireman.

There was a new notice on the bulletin board, signed by MacKenzie. It said the child rape victim was better but not conscious yet. He wasn't there for a ride home but she found a note in her box with his phone number.

Leaving, her eyes went to the suspect's picture once again, stark black on white, the crazy eyes. He'd kicked a dog to death and raped a little girl. He was real. He wasn't just a sick picture anymore.

She picked MacKenzie up now in the mornings. The mornings of their "days" that began before midnight.

He didn't chatter going down into the city, but he talked some and she got to know him. Two grown sons and a daughter. The oldest son, with two degrees in engineering, getting dirty on the oil rigs in Alaska. Working his way up in an oil company that started young executives at the bottom. The other roaming across the country with a friend and a guitar deciding what comes next. Probably another college. And the daughter about to have a baby in Santa Rosa.

She realized he'd heard her fuss about her uniforms when one day he handed her a business card. "A little German tailor in the Tenderloin. Most people in the bureaus use him. He's good with clothes for both men and women but he seems to know the difference. Give him the lot, shirts and all. He keeps the door locked so you'll have to knock and wait where he can see you."

Carrie said with a sigh, "Sometimes I get the feeling all these lumps are me."

She told him of Alkron's inside dope about his search for the rapist in the Southern and he laughed when he heard what Spenser had said. "I'd like to meet the man. We could use someone around here who could apply common sense to department rumors."

She told him most of her friends were anxious to get into the bureaus. "Status, I suppose, and to stop working nights."

MacKenzie said, "I didn't have a choice. After my wife died I had to be at home nights with the children. The department let me start in traffic investigation, and I had some luck with a couple of hard cases."

She'd heard that before. "Dumb luck," Bullard said. "Only good cops have dumb luck."

"Now I'd rather be in uniform," he said. "I don't mind the hours. People are a little more themselves at odd hours."

They had comfortable silences when they didn't talk at all.

One night he'd paused with the door open and waved an arm back at his redwood house set into a stand of firs. "This is something else that changed when the children all grew up. I traded the big family house for this. It's all glass on the other side, looking down into the canyon."

He slid in. "I used to patrol these streets, up this little mountain. I'd drive up at least once on every watch. A private canyon hidden in the middle of a city. Up here we'd get calls about raccoons thieving out of garbage cans. One night I stopped and turned off the lights to listen. There was some reason, I don't remember what. When I switched them on again this family of rabbits was sitting in the road.

"Then all I saw was rabbit tails."

She laughed, tempted for a moment to make a turn and go up his roadway.

"I'll show you some night if you want to see. We might even spot a possum. Now and then we smell a skunk. One night some frightened New Yorkers thought they saw a bear and wanted us to come flush it out. We came up and made a little noise and told them the bear had run away. So they could go back to sleep."

He talked about vacations in the Sierras, camping out near a trout stream with the children. She told him of fishing days on the beach with Spenser. How they watched the sea birds to know where the striped bass were.

"When I was small I could never cast out far enough. We could see the gulls diving after the bait fish and I thought if I could get just a little farther, and I'd tell Spenser we had to have a boat. But that's not for Spenser. He was happy just standing there and casting out, and he always got a bass for dinner, and sometimes one to freeze.

"Not me. I'd keep inching out until I was swimming, all tangled up in my line, and he'd come out and carry me in, sometimes with a fish attached. Then we'd have to straighten out the mess."

It was easy, talking to MacKenzie. She thought, It's like riding down with Spenser. And watched him from the corner of her eye, square-jawed and slim.

Downtown, his lineups didn't become perfunctory.

The night after the fire, he said, "The child shows signs

of increasing vitality. She's no longer in a coma. It's more like a deep sleep. It's a good sign, I'm told. Her doctors are able to detect signs of muscular activity, when she responds to a family voice or a loud sound. Afterward she appears to lapse back into nearly normal sleep. Her parents take turns sitting with her, along with Inspector Hendry.

"On the bad side, they're concerned that the bruises on her back might mean a spinal injury. This means she could recover only to become a cripple.

"Once again, please do not telephone. They're getting more calls than they can handle. Most of them from police officers."

Of the firebug, he said, "There is no reason to suppose he'll stay in the Mission. All he needs is a wood house and accumulated trash and newspapers and a match. Please report any trash piles you think are candidates for setting fires. We'll have them cleaned up.

"There is no description of a suspect. Firemen have not spotted anyone loitering near a fire scene. Apparently, unlike some arsonists, he is satisfied to light his fire and walk away."

Then the night's stolen cars and crimes and descriptions of criminals.

And the litany:

"Hats will be worn. Summer uniforms, no jackets. Please remember we have a deputy chief who does not sleep well after midnight and likes to patrol in his personal car. He has an abiding interest in correct dress, especially hats. I'm sure you all have a description of his car.

"Do not be caught without your hat, or be prepared to lose two days' pay or to stand before the captain and explain the absence of your hat, if that is the way you wish to spend your weekends."

In good, clear, precise department language.

Five radio cars and a wagon, twelve men and women and one sergeant and an acting lieutenant who liked the streets, and a station keeper to pick up the jangling phone and run license plates on the computer, and a lineup room like a cave set into the middle of a jumble of rooms and offices. Inside a building that stood gray and square from sidewalk to sidewalk on a whole city block, where a baseball field once stood that graduated players into the big leagues, three of them into the baseball Hall of Fame, before the city decided they could build another playground somewhere else. But never did.

The door of the lineup room opened into the long central corridor in the building, far from the street. The other bureaus and courtrooms were on the next four floors above, and above them two floors of jail. It made escape difficult, and sometimes fatal, but not impossible.

The district stations were set around the city. The older ones were roomier. Richmond Station, an ornate red brick barracks on a residential street, still had a barn out back for horses that smelled of old leather and old hay. The station captain kept his sports car in it.

Station officers there had an exercise room in the loft, and a big room with a kitchen for heating fancy dinners wives would sometimes bring from home. Old residents on that block remembered a day when policemen would gallop their horses over the city streets to pull up and begin a stately patrol through Golden Gate Park.

MacKenzie said he would resume the occasional barbecue in the back parking lot and would donate his barbecue with a spit for turning meat if someone would go get it. "I'm temporarily without a car. Until my daughter decides to have a baby. Then maybe I'll get it back." He looked out at them and smiled. "And maybe I won't."

They drifted out to their cars. Alkron was riding with Carrie until Roger used up some overtime. The four-car sector was a rectangle in the middle of the Southern, from Market Street south to the boundary of the Potrero, four blocks across, each one as long as two ordinary city blocks. Its residents spanned the socioeconomic gamut from powerful newspaper owner to the lowest echelons, in the old hotels and unpainted wood Victorians and residential warehouses, some to die there, young or old, some to work their way uptown or out into the avenues.

"Our constituents," Alkron said, "will never see polished floors. Except when they come to court, if it happens to be a third Tuesday of the month. With their luck, they'll miss that, too."·

Alkron liked to drive. "How do you like our widower lieutenant soon to be captain? He put his hands on you yet?"

"Why me?" Carrie asked, surprised.

"You're a sexy bit," Alkron told her. "The boys call you the Olympic sex symbol. Sleek and slim."

"Come on, Alkron." She was annoyed. "I'm nobody's sex symbol."

"No. You're just beautiful. They talk but they don't touch. That's why I asked about MacKenzie. He's another one who doesn't fool around. The serious type, like you."

"You're the second person in a week to tell me I was beautiful. My uncle said so, too."

But it shocked her a little. That wasn't her picture of herself. Shoulders too broad, hips too big, too much bottom even for these pants.

But Alkron sighed and said seriously, "Oh, Lubick, if I had your looks I wouldn't have to play the field. I've got to keep two or three hot after me so if one of them gets married to some girl I never heard of it won't break me up. Mine are always going off to marry someone else. I don't know where they find them. They all look like they come out of church choirs, and the guys I date don't go to church. At least, they don't talk to me about it."

They went through the sector twice, pausing once to send a family in a mobile home off the bridge at Islais Creek to a legal parking place near the station, under brighter streetlights.

"Keep the doors locked and the windows mostly closed," Carrie told them. "Cities aren't that safe at night." Knowing they probably wouldn't.

They patrolled on foot together when the bars shut down, this time going the other way around, up past the Greyhound and along the arcades on Market, then down Sixth Street to the sidewalk shoe and boot emporium, closed now.

Out of the car, on the open street, Alkron's manner changed. Her warmth left her. She became abrupt, her voice harsher. When she said, "Move it," the street people looked up, surprised.

"You like this crap," she said. "You've got a reputation for it. I just feel exposed. I'm for the bureaus and civilian clothes. With luck, I can maneuver it. I got promises. The trouble is, it's always before, not after." She shrugged. "That's the game."

Then she grinned broadly. "Well, it's my game and I like it. All my future husbands are going to be cops."

Carrie often thought of Alkron and her friends, protesting to herself that there wasn't any joy in it. Now she thought, She brings her own joy to it, and liked Alkron for that. And envied her a little.

"Come on, Lubick, let's hump it. We've got an hour before lunch. Maybe something will happen to make me shine like an inspector."

They rode the sector. It was quiet. Car windows open, listening to the radio, eyes on the street. They kept tabs on Washoe, riding by himself. "He doesn't like it but he won't admit it. He likes another body. That says it. He's not afraid of anything, just doesn't like to be alone. I got him figured out."

On the other side, Ed Wellington rode with a new partner named Lawrence Kang. The two radio cars met at the new Hotel Meridien and parked behind a lone taxi. The hotel was quiet, too. No ball gowns tonight.

"I don't know where my street people are," Wellington said. "There's no one sleeping on the sidewalks. It isn't time for government checks so they can't be in the hotels. I don't know where they've gone."

"You miss 'em?" Alkron asked.

He smiled. "They come with the streets. I'm supposed to watch 'em. In the winter, the mayor wants me to count 'em."

Lawrence Kang leaned around Wellington to say, "I think we'd better move along. The better hotels don't want us sitting around like paid security. It's not subtle. You know, nice people don't need policemen."

They all looked at him.

"I used to work in the Central," he said. "I learned the finer points."

They moved on, Carrie driving, twisting through the alleys. Hot enough but no heat wave. She kept Alkron's heavy hand off the flood. Alkron complained, "I can't see in the corners."

"Nothing's moving. Let's not wake everybody up."

Showing the flag. Black and white. Wellington was right. It was too quiet. It made her uneasy, too.

They headed in, past the fenced corner of the schoolyard. Even the commuter rush, four lanes across, like an army, seemed innocent of trouble. She saw Wellington across the parking lot. They looked at one another, shrugged.

They had their quirks, her streets, her people.

She was sitting in a summer robe, her windows open to the ocean breeze, writing a letter to her sister when the phone rang. MacKenzie said, "Can you pick me up? We ought to start an hour early. Bob Poggi wants to see me in the Taraval."

"I'm almost ready," she said. "Be there in half an hour."

She was reminding Jennie of the time the kite got stuck in the big elm tree near their house when she was eleven. She'd gone up the elm, thirty feet above the ground, because her sister and the other little kids had come to her to get it down. Afterward that strange woman down the street called her the neighborhood tough guy. She'd waited to ask Spenser.

"Did she mean I'm not going to be a woman?"

Spenser said, "I suppose that's what she meant, if a fool means anything. I think it's a mistake to be hurt by someone like that, but if it hurts, let's talk about it. Why did you climb the tree?"

"Well, Uncle Spenser." The question exasperated her. "The damn kite was there. Who else was going to get it down?"

He grinned. "No one, I guess, except you. It's your neighborhood."

She got the point, though. He was right. She wouldn't have wanted someone else to do it.

"Okay," she said. "Do you see me as some kind of boy?"

He smiled. "Not in the least. You're one of the most feminine people I know. I know the woman who said it, too, and I suspect some malice there. But let's keep thrashing at it. What about the tree? Were you afraid?"

That startled her. "Sure. I was higher than the house, and when I got up there I found the blackberry vines ran all the way and I had to inch through them. Look, I've still got scratches." She held out her arms.

"Were you afraid of falling?"

She'd laughed. "No, I was too busy picking the next place for my hands and feet, and trying to squeeze through those vines. I knew I'd have to remember how to get back the same way. The handholds look different going down. And those blackberries were cutting me to pieces."

"All right," he said, "you kept your mind on your business and didn't fall and break your neck. And you got the kite."

"I got it, all right, and I sent that thing skimming down like a giant Frisbee! And you know what else, Uncle Spenser? You can see half the roofs in town up there. You get a feeling of glory!"

He waited through that little outburst and he said, "I don't see what this has to do with womanhood, do you? I don't see the connection. If you do, let me know."

She said, "I guess there isn't any, is there?"

"None at all," Spenser said, and his voice, his face, his certainty had set her free to do so many things she might not have done otherwise.

This job, for instance. "I'm picking places for my hands and feet again, in a blue uniform," she told her sister, "and liking it. I guess I haven't changed much since eleven. So much for the fine-honing of a good university, and the influence of a bright sister, not to mention a literate uncle."

She pulled her small schoolteacher's car into the midnight streets and thought ahead to where MacKenzie waited in his soft blues, his graying hair, hat tucked under his arm. Then her mind was back on the traffic trying to crowd her off the street. She shouldered through. Macho drivers in shiny cars gave way at the last moment for her yellow Toyota but it took concentration. He was there waiting for her.

"Bob Poggi says it's urgent. Something about our rapist. I thought you might want to sit in."

She remembered talk at the academy about Sergeant Poggi, who ran his own show on the midnight watches in the Taraval. His new officers played games with him, tried to find a street he didn't know, a building he couldn't place. By the time they'd finished teaching him his district there wasn't much they didn't know about it, and they covered it like ski troops flying down a mountain.

Poggi sat at the lieutenant's desk under a high, frescoed ceiling. Two officers were with him, both women. One short, one tall, their hats and sticks on the floor beside their chairs. They got up to be introduced. Officers Leong and Kedrick. Then they all sat down.

"I've got a problem I hope you can help me with." Poggi was tall, too, his eyes sharp, his hair just over regulation length. "This used to be your case, MacKenzie. If you were in the bureau, I'd have phoned, or sent a scratch, but I don't know those guys in the bureau. Here's a scratch I did for the captain, in case I decide to give it to him. I made copies before the machine broke down again."

He passed out copies. He talked while they read.

"I'll have to have someone run over to the Richmond to copy our reports. If their machine is working. Luscomb's got a good one over at the Ingleside. I don't know where he gets the good equipment. He's got a graft somewhere. Anyway, he won't let us use it.

"It's like the war," he said to Carrie. "If you wanted a deep-freeze that worked, you stole it from the Seabees. The rest of the time, you were on the same side."

She was reading. "This is to notify the captain that two of our officers assigned to the one-car sector may have uncovered evidence of importance in the ongoing investigation of the sexual assaults perpetrated in the districts bordering the Taraval—the Richmond, the Park and the Northern."

She lifted her eyes from the page and looked at the two women. They were looking sheepish. The tall blonde, Kedrick, shuffled her feet in her slip-proof shoes. It wasn't easy to do.

"The problem is," Poggi said, "we may have found something, but if we did, it was found by two officers who had no business being where they were at the time they found it. If it turns out to be important to the case, I would put them up for at least a captain's citation or perhaps a commendation, but if I do, the captain is going to ask me if there was some reason one of our radio cars, on my watch, was halfway across the city in a neighboring district. Twice."

MacKenzie smiled. "I understand. What did they find?"

"An old car. These two officers ran in on two of our early rapes. They have a car, the same car, parked within two blocks of each crime location.

"Now, we have the further complication of the time. It took them a month to find out what they had. Now, this discovery of theirs may not be important enough to the investigation to risk the displeasure of the captain and the possible filing of a reprimand, to be placed in their personnel jackets. We three are agreed, however, that if it is important, we should risk the reprimand in light of the serious nature of these crimes. I said we should consult you, and if you don't like the information, no harm done."

Poggi sat back. He'd made his case.

MacKenzie said, "We knocked on all the doors. For two blocks around. I don't know what might have been discovered since, but when I left the bureau, all we had was frightened victims. No witnesses at all. You'd better tell me what you have."

Poggi sighed. "We have a red car, parked a short walk from each crime scene. Within minutes of the time the calls came in. Twice. The same car. The same plates.

"I'd better explain. We play a game out here. Officer Leong made it up. We drive down a street and pick a block. The officer who is not driving watches the cars parked along the curb. Later, say, in a coffee shop, she makes a list. All the cars, plates, color, dented fenders. All from memory. Officer Leong gets every one. In the order they were parked. I have never seen her make an error. Sometimes we ask her to do two blocks."

Leong, the small one, shuffled her feet, too. Now they

were both doing it. She said, "I think it's my Oriental mind."

Poggi said, "We have to remember that in this case, she saw a car almost as old as she is. This may cast some doubt on her identification of a 1969 Ford."

Officer Leong said sharply, "I know those cars very well. My uncle had one. I saw it a lot of times."

He waved her to be silent. "I should also add," he said, "that Officer Leong has already found three stolen cars by checking her list with the hot sheet afterward, which is unusual, as you know, because stolen cars are not left in the Taraval. They are stolen in the Taraval and left in the Potrero or the Ingleside."

Officer Leong interrupted. "I have to look at it on paper before I get the connection. That's my weakness. I have to write it first. My mind doesn't pick it up right away when I see the car." She added, "The way it should."

MacKenzie smiled at that. He asked, "Each time it was parked within two blocks?"

She nodded. "I can show you on the map. I can mark the parking places."

"I'll ask you to do that for me now," MacKenzie said. "You ran the plates?"

"We did," Poggi said. "A woman in Santa Rosa. Except the plates belong to a gray 1967 Chevrolet. Not a red 1969 Ford. We don't know who belongs to Leong's car."

"Nor do we know," MacKenzie said, "that there's a connection with our crimes."

Leong objected, "But it was so clear, each time. It really stood out. As if it was important!"

"Look at it this way," Poggi said. "Someone has

parked his car within a short walk from two crime scenes, a mile apart, on the nights those crimes were committed. Why did he do that? Maybe he jogs to his home from somewhere in the Golden Gate Park every night, and the next morning jogs back again to get in his car and go to work. People are strange, and I can even buy that. But he's got the wrong plates on his car and he's got to know it."

"I don't disagree with you," MacKenzie said. "I want to know more about it. The Santa Rosa woman, does she have a current driver's license?"

"Yes. She's fifty-two and overweight, tall for a woman but still fat, no warrants, no unpaid parking tickets. I've got a street address. She owns no other car. Just this old four-door Chevrolet. No red Ford."

"I see your point," MacKenzie said. "You can't do much more from here."

MacKenzie said, "It took you a long time to come up with this. You're talking about two crimes in the Richmond District in mid-June and early July and it's the middle of August now. Why so long?"

"It was the little girl," Kedrick said. "That got to us. We took a break and stopped for a cup of coffee. We talked about what would have happened if that little girl lived in our neighborhood, and she wanted help and we were halfway across town. We already talked about those old women, you know, like, where were the beat cars over there, what were those guys doing they let those old women get knocked around and raped right in their neighborhoods, and then we said, 'Yeah, sure, big talk. Where were we?'

"So," Kedrick went on, "we sat down and Leong made her lists. The two crime nights. And there it was, the same red Ford. So we came in and looked for Sergeant Poggi. Now you're here. I guess it's real."

Sergeant Poggi looked at his old friend. "All right, Ian. Is this important? If it is, what do I do with it?"

"Send in your scratch," MacKenzie said. "And prepare to write a detailed report, and get it downtown to the bureau. Get the captain to initial it. You know the way."

Poggi sighed again. "Yeah. I know. So if there's heat, we handle it. I'll think of something. I'll come down and see the captain later. Lay it out. Who knows? I could have sent them over there to cover. That was a long time ago.

"Actually, I think that's what happened. I sent them over there and the channel was snarled up with calls for the ambulance and the crime lab and all that. I thought I heard someone acknowledge. Maybe I was wrong."

"Keep it simple," MacKenzie told him. Smiling.

"Yeah, that's what you always said when we worked together. Command officers do not always wish to be bothered with unpleasant truths. Make it easy for them. Only it used to be sergeants we said that about."

MacKenzie said, "Discipline isn't what it used to be."

"It never was," Poggi said.

Outside, they all walked toward Carrie's car, parked at the edge of a vast, dark park, and she smelled the mown grass. There was air to breathe. It wasn't like downtown.

"You ought to transfer out with us," Kedrick said.

Carrie smiled at that. "I like the Southern. I've got a getaway in Forestville. I go there weekends to be civilized."

Leong said, "One thing. I said it stood out. Nothing easy like a banged-up side panel or a twisted bumper. It had new tires. On that old car like my uncle used to drive. Big black shiny brand new tires. And nothing under them. No windblown trash. That car was just perched there, ready to move out. It called my name. 'Leong, over here!' Twice. I don't know how to put that in a report."

MacKenzie said, "Just leave out the bit about the voice. This is not going to be universally believed downtown, but that's where it's got to go."

"All right," Poggi said. "We go the whole nine yards."

Downtown, Carrie joined Roger for the watch. He drove and she sat with the clipboard in her lap, flashlight on the list of stolen cars, watching the parked cars. She couldn't remember two plates in a row.

Word came in the middle of a watch. MacKenzie had a grandson. At four A.M. Carrie and Roger drove through the flower mart, winding through the trucks unloading the day's potted plants and cut flowers for the city's curbside flower stands and flower shops. They collected a bunch of cut summer flowers and the flower merchant stopped unloading long enough to find an old white vase. It had a crack in it, but it held water. When they carried it into the station Wellington was there with a box of cigars from a news vendor's stand just opening downtown. With pink wrappers. "I'd take them home and dye the wrappers but I'd throw up smelling those cigars," Alkron said.

They'd all warmed to MacKenzie. He might be a little quiet, a little stern, but he was theirs.

"I'm going to buy the kid his first hat," Washoe said. "Then I'm going to make him wear it."

MacKenzie put a note on the bulletin board. "Beef ribs on me tomorrow night. I need someone with a wagon to bring down the barbecue."

Alkron scrawled across it "potato salad." Carrie thought of the container in her refrigerator filled with tomatoes from Rosalee's garden and wrote "tomatoes" and "paper towels."

Gillespie, the big ex-fireman, came in for station relief and said, "Every time it was my turn to cook we had a three-alarm fire. They made me stop cooking. But if you guys will take a chance, I'll volunteer."

MacKenzie stopped Carrie as she was going to the car. "I'm meeting with the two inspectors from sex crimes. They have Poggi's memo. It only took a day for the captain to think it over and send it downtown." He smiled at that. "I was afraid he'd just file it. I told them I'd stay late. They said they'll come in early, if you'd like to hear the other shoe drop."

She said she would. "I'll wait by your office. Will one of them be big and one small?"

"I think that's the department order."

"I guess I'll know them."

She added, "Congratulations."

The smile in his eyes went deep. He just said, "I'll have to find the kids' old fishing poles. I'm not sure where I put them when I moved."

"But you say you never throw anything of theirs away."

"That's right. I guess I don't."

She told Roger later, in the car. "Did you know that MacKenzie is a fisherman?" And thought to herself, Lubick, you're getting positively giddy. What's wrong with you? Roger smiled. He'd say something when he had something to say. They rode and looked out the open windows.

MacKenzie was waiting for her with the two inspectors outside the glassed-in cubicle where the day-watch lieutenant was sorting out his papers. They went down for coffee. McKitrick and Gallina, in sport coats. Gallina was the little one, about her size. They sat around the small round table in the basement cafeteria over coffee that grew lukewarm while they talked. The two men kept their faces closed.

"Gallina doesn't like your red car," McKitrick told MacKenzie. "But we're checking. We sent a Teletype to Santa Rosa requesting that they check it out. The state computer says the woman has owned one car in twenty years. It isn't red. That's as far back as they go. Before that, someone has to go up to Sacramento and shuffle papers. An older woman. Probably just some screwup and she never noticed. It doesn't look like anything, but we're checking."

Looking at their faces, she felt she was intruding, but she asked, "Do you have anyone who saw a car at all?"

"Only in the last one," McKitrick said. "Three cars,

all moving, somewhere in the eight-block area we covered, going door to door. Two compacts, one full-size, brown, a new car. That's all. Nothing fits."

"Nothing on the occupants?" MacKenzie asked.

"Our witnesses can barely remember the cars," Gallina said. "We already talked to them twice. Maybe one of them made up a car, just to get rid of us. That leaves two. I don't think there's anything in this red car."

"Have you got anything solid at all?" MacKenzie asked.

"Not much, Ian," McKitrick said. "Bits and pieces. We've spent hours in the neighborhoods. We've seen the same people so often they invite us in for coffee."

"I've seen pictures of a million grandchildren," Gallina said.

McKitrick said, "We're going over files with juvenile. We want every kid who ever poked a dog with a stick to make it bleed. For the past ten years. We're talking to California Parole people. We've got every sex offender who's been let out near here in the past five years. We've talked to the school nurses and the school psychologists. I'm getting the idea we've got a new one, someone who just surfaced. He's going to make us work."

Carrie asked, "Isn't there some physical evidence? He was inside some of those homes, wasn't he?"

Gallina looked at her with his closed face. "It's on the Teletypes. More you don't need to know."

MacKenzie said, "You're still uncertain about the composite. You're still asking the newspapers to hold off, or I'd have seen them. They wanted to use them right away."

McKitrick sighed. "Even one of our victims says it isn't the same guy. She just shakes her head. Except it's the same guy. But if we missed a blemish on his nose we'd ruin ourselves in court. Maybe he's only got one ear and they saw two.

"Those victims. You know them. They're old and full of fear. Little old ladies. They think they sinned."

"If the child lives . . ." MacKenzie began.

"Yeah. Then we might get something," McKitrick agreed. "Children are good. They see things. But who's going to tell her about her dog?" The big man looked sad. "I don't want the job."

Carrie walked side-by-side with MacKenzie out the door to the parking lot. They both paused at the new watch list. She turned the page back to appointments to lieutenant. Ian MacKenzie. Acting Lieutenant to Lieutenant.

She said, "Are you glad? It's pretty final, isn't it?"

"The kids are on their own. It's where I want to be."

"You have to watch while your old friends upstairs go round and round with your old case. Isn't that frustrating?"

"No. They'll get a break. You keep going over the same ground then someone remembers something."

"Like the red car."

MacKenzie said, "Like that. I called Bob Poggi before we left the station. Gave him today to find an old red car. Tonight, he can have his troops drive it out there under those new streetlights. We don't know what those new lights will do."

"You mean, see if it looks brown. I didn't think of that."

"We've got eight blocks of those new lights. Patrol units in the Richmond have been complaining there's a color change. We need to know what colors change.

"Our witness really might have seen a dignified old red Ford with bright chrome trim and shiny new black tires."

"Like some new cars," she said.

"Like some new cars," he agreed. "Trust Poggi. He'll find a red car covered with street dust, then see what it looks like under the new lights.

"Then we look at the rest of it. Someone get our witness out of bed in the middle of the night. Maybe we'll know then why a witness saw a new car out of the corner of his eye."

Carrie told him, "I'd never have put all that together."

"It's not hard. I had good teachers, older police officers, when I was new, wanted me to raise my children. They saw to it that I had a chance to do it. I didn't have to work nights and weekends. We were a good family. Now it's my turn to pay back."

"You fished," she said. "Did you take them?"

"Every time. We went back to the mountain streams

I fished as a boy. Up there, you don't count the fish. You eat the fish for dinner and lie there and count the stars."

When he opened the car door, she said, "I'm driving up to my uncle's house this weekend. I could drop you at the hospital or wherever your car is."

He said, "I'd like that. Maybe I'll meet your uncle."

She watched him up the walk to his own place. A little redwood house in a forest of fir and redwood, on this hill.

Carrie, she told herself firmly, you are very tired and your mind has turned to dishwater, and she drove down the hill.

Half the watch was chewing ribs and dripping sauce on their shoes, wearing Washoe's funny hats, when Boy Four was called. Roger hit the bump at the driveway exit, already turning, MacKenzie right behind. "Woman screaming. Possible two-sixty-one." A rape. "Check if an ambulance is needed," headquarters said. Carrie didn't like these in the best of times. Now it gave her a cold shiver.

Cars with women officers weren't sent by choice. Any

car would do. Besides, some victims didn't want a woman officer. They wanted someone like MacKenzie, with graying hair, or Roger, whose eyes weren't accusing. A young woman was there, in the headlights, sitting on the curb, wiping her eyes with a pair of black panties. Lace and all. In jeans and shirt and purple leather sneakers. Rocking back and forth and moaning, "Oh, my God, he raped me! Oh, my God!" Hugging herself across her stomach. Carrie sat on the curb and put an arm around her shoulders.

An excited East Indian stood beside the girl. "I called!" he told them. "I called the police!"

Carrie held the girl with one arm and reached down to button the oversize man's shirt she was wearing, pulling it together over her breasts. No brassiere. No scratches or bruises there, either. A bruise was growing around the girl's left eye.

"My stomach!" the girl moaned. "He kicked me in the stomach!"

"He has violated her in my hotel. I'm Patel, the manager," the East Indian was saying. "I saw him run out! He is not staying at my hotel! The girl is not staying with me, either! I do not know these people!"

Roger walked the East Indian up the street, notebook out.

MacKenzie asked Carrie, "Any bites or marks?"

"No. I looked. Except her eye."

She kept a firm pressure on the girl's shoulders. "Are you hurt anywhere else?" Still rocking and moaning. "He kicked me and he raped me! Isn't that enough, for God's sake?"

The ambulance pulled up. Carrie pulled the girl to her feet. "He was black and his name was Ronald. He's a guard at the Greyhound. He said he wears a gun when he's in uniform but I didn't see it. He said he had some good stuff and we could have a smoke," the girl said. "Then the bastard kicked me!"

The steward and the medic took the girl.

Roger came back with his notebook. "He was maybe twenty, wore light blue pants, shirt the same. Short natural, blue running shoes. No marks or scars that Patel could see. He only saw him running through the lobby, then the girl came down screaming."

"Put it out," MacKenzie said. Roger used the car radio, asked headquarters to send a Central car to check the other side of Market. "We'll do this side," he said. "Two blocks east and west of Seventh Street. You might ask the other cars to check the rest, in case he's a strong runner."

They set out walking, MacKenzie on the other side, checking bars, arcades, cheap clothing stores with sidewalk displays. Walked through restrooms, kicked open the stall doors.

Customers asked, "What did he do?"

"We just want him. Young, black, maybe twenty, short natural, blue leisure suit, running shoes."

They'd go back later, look again, in case he'd gotten himself squirreled away in a coat closet they'd missed.

MacKenzie crossed over to them. They walked back to get their cars. Roger said, "We don't even know which room they used. I guess he borrowed it, or broke in."

They parked near the double doors of Central Emergency. The sexual trauma cases were brought here, unless they were badly hurt. Then they went to General Hospital.

Cars were reporting in from Market Street. No one had found him.

Other cars were sent to the ends of the two cable car lines, to bus stops in the Haight and the Castro.

"I've just got her first name," Carrie said. "Linda. She lives in Walnut Creek. Came to the city with a girlfriend. That's all I learned."

Linda's first name was printed neatly on the log for sexual traumas, restricted, to separate it from the other injured. To keep it private. Which only means, Roger told her once, that you can never find them if they get shifted to another hospital. "So you're walking around with a suspect in handcuffs and you can't find the victim."

The head nurse said dryly, "She was most cooperative. She even gave me her real name, I think. Her father is a very important man over there, a councilman or commissioner or something."

Linda hadn't made a hit in here.

They stood in the white-tiled hallway with its wooden benches. Sometimes it took an hour or more. They had to wait for the reports, the smears, lab tests. Take back the evidence. The underwear, if that was pertinent. Whatever. For the trial. MacKenzie waited with them.

Linda walked out with a nurse, a doctor. She went straight to Roger. Her clothes were buttoned and her face was washed, her brown hair brushed. She looked young and imperious.

"I don't want my father told," she told Roger.

"If you're eighteen, we don't have to tell your father," Roger said. "I'll have to see it."

"Of course I'm eighteen," Linda said. "And you'll be

terribly sorry if you upset my father over this. I'm not a bit certain it was rape. He was unable to complete the act."

She didn't look at Carrie. She spoke to Roger and MacKenzie.

Roger said, "You're going to have an awful shiner."

Carrie quietly cheered Roger. The doctor took her by the arm, out of hearing. "She won't see the trauma counselor. She has a lot of friends to talk to who understand these things. So she says. You've got plenty of semen if you want it. We'll get a blood type out of it. You've got a stiff poke in the eye. I guess you've got an assault, too, if you want it. It's my guess she won't back you on the rape, but the evidence will. Force and violence, all that."

He handed her the sealed envelope with the case number outside. Carrie made a note of that.

Roger and MacKenzie were listening to Linda from Walnut Creek. "I think you've misconstrued the whole thing." Roger had his notebook out. "We met these boys in the arcade with the tall green sign. Ronald was good-looking and I let him talk to me. He seemed very nice. Not just another city colored boy, you know, smart talk and all.

"When he said he had some good stuff in his hotel, why I naturally thought it would be all right, but when we got inside he just knocked me around and I ran out. Frankly, I don't think he had any stuff there at all!"

Carrie said, "You forgot the sexual assault. You said raped, sitting out there on the curb."

Linda turned to MacKenzie. "I was sure she was going to misconstrue the whole thing. I said distinctly I was kicked in the stomach, and that's all I said!"

"I know," MacKenzie said. "I was there."

Roger asked her, "Do you know where your girlfriend is?"

"I'm sure she just drove home. That's what we do. If one of us meets a friend or something."

"Won't your parents worry when you're late?"

"At my age? They stopped worrying about me ages ago."

"How will you get home?"

"My boyfriend will come and pick me up, if you've got a telephone." Linda reached into a tight back pocket and brought out a soft leather wallet. "I'll pay for the call."

The nurse led her to the telephone. "Free to all rape victims. Usually they get robbed, too. You were lucky."

When she was through, Roger handed her a page from his notebook. "There's my name and Officer Lubick's. The case number, in case you'd like to pick up a copy of the report. It will all be there. When there's an arrest, you'll be asked to make an identification. The sex crimes detail will call. The district attorney will contact you when you need to come and testify."

Linda was uneasy. "I don't know what I'd testify to."

"Just what you told us. It will be in the report."

She was worried now. "I don't think my father will stand for this notoriety," but she'd lost her haughtiness. She sat on a bench.

Outside, MacKenzie said, "I'll send the crime lab to get pictures of that eye."

"We'll stay until the boyfriend comes," Carrie said. "I'd rather not leave her alone."

"Not with that nurse," Roger said.

Later, they watched a newish Mercury station wagon turn in, a young man at the wheel. He sounded his horn. Linda slid into the seat.

Carrie was disgusted. "My feelings were raped and I don't like it."

Roger cruised past the now closing arcades on Market Street once more. No blue leisure suit.

"You remember the old wino in the service station restroom?" Roger asked her. "She forgot about her rape when we got her bottle back."

"She couldn't go back to Walnut Creek," Carrie said.

Roger said, "Let's write the report."

Going in, they met MacKenzie.

Carrie said, "I've got a question. You asked me about bite marks. Why bite marks?"

MacKenzie studied her. "Our rapist. We didn't put it on the Teletypes. He kicks and bites. Apparently, he likes to bite to draw blood. He's done that three times. He did it to the child." He paused. "He bit her on the ear. He nearly bit it off."

It was Monday night. MacKenzie stood at the lineup, smiling at them all as they sorted themselves out and became quiet.

"First, for those of you who haven't already heard it on the radio or seen it on television, our young rape victim is now conscious. There do not seem to be the spinal injuries they feared. Also, she was not raped. That earlier assumption was made because of massive bruising. She was kicked and pummeled, but not raped."

"She's not conscious for long periods. She keeps drifting back into sleep again. But she's on the mend. There isn't any question now but that she'll live."

He let them shuffle around while he sorted pieces of paper, then waved them quiet.

"Tonight is the two-week anniversary of the assault on her, in the Northern. All three districts where these crimes have occurred will be at full strength. This rapist strikes at two-week intervals, though once it was four weeks. Three times on Monday nights, once on a Tuesday night. We don't cover those neighborhoods where he's found his victims in the past, but be watchful."

He read routine announcements.

"As for fires, we haven't had the arson problem in the Southern, either, but keep making note of obvious piles of combustibles. They'll be picked up in the mornings."

The cars bumped out into the street. The channels had some excited chitchat on the little girl. "I'm taking that kid dancing." That was Washoe. Headquarters let it go. Soon it died away, but Carrie felt a lightness in the air. It had been missing for a while.

Headquarters broke in. "Boy Two, please go to Mission and Third streets. Traffic light is out. The Department of Electricity has been notified. Their ETA is twenty minutes. Boy Five, please respond to a traffic accident, Eleventh at Howard. Check if an ambulance is needed.''

And added, ''We would also like to say hooray.''

In that flat voice.

That set them off again and headquarters responded with a barrage of low-priority assignments. They never seemed to stop. She and Roger found couples dancing outside the arcades on Market Street where someone had turned a speaker to full volume. They worked straight through their normal period for lunch. All two-bit troubles.

They helped sort out a fight in a bar out of their sector and shoved two men into the wagon. Roger picked up the mike to tell headquarters where they were, that they were coming in to book two prisoners, write reports.

''Are you on Twelfth Street, Boy Four? Go over one. Check a smell of smoke outside a warehouse at Howard and Thirteenth.'' Roger turned. They could both smell it. ''Confirmed,'' Carrie said into the mike as Roger turned hard into Thirteenth Street, then saw a glint of flames over the warehouse, down an alley. ''We have an on-view fire.'' She gave the location. Roger braked into the alley mouth, filling up with smoke ahead of them, and she shouted, ''My God, Roger, there's that damned red car!''

But they were past, flames visible in front of them roaring up the side of a wooden three-story house, a warren of apartments in this alley, Roger bumping up onto the sidewalk. They were both out, running up the concrete steps. No fire in front as yet but burning down the side, smoke rolling out of the front door. A man stumbled out carrying a child, a woman in a nightgown clutching him with one hand. A man behind them, wearing only his pants. He bellowed, "We're all out! The first floor!" And waved them up the stairs. She couldn't see the flames but heard the roar. She was ahead of Roger. She turned the corner and ran up the third flight of stairs and heard Roger below, pounding on the doors and shouting.

She heard sirens in the alley, the deep tone of the fire siren shutting down. Right outside. Not much smoke up here, but the roar of flames drummed at the air from somewhere. She pounded on a door, then drew back and kicked it open with her foot, one solid blow at the latch. It flew open and she was almost blinded by a wall of flame across the room, roaring upward from the windows. The heat seared her face and eyes. In the red light she saw forms huddled beneath a blanket on a bed. She stumbled over a wine bottle, caught herself and kicked at the low bed, shouting, "Get up! Get out of here!" The forms stirred and the blanket was thrown back. She grabbed an arm and pulled. A naked girl stumbled out of the bedclothes, then a naked man. The windows exploded flame, curling all across the ceiling. She held them and shouted, "Children! Babies! Do you have any babies?"

The man shouted, "Next door!" and pointed. She shoved them to the door and toward the stairs, in the smoke, in all the roar, then turned for the other door, her eyes streaming now with tears and her chest bursting with the smoke that burned in her throat. She felt the door with her hand, then the doorknob, and drew back and kicked again, once, twice with that shoe that seemed so light now, felt the door give and stumbled inside into blackness, and just stood there, unable to see where to go next. Then a ceiling light came on. Two people in a bed.

She swept back the blankets. A man and woman, and a child. She reached out and took it in her arms. Blond hair. A little girl. She swept her up, blanket and all, and found Roger at her side. His mouth formed a scream. "The drapes are going!" She turned, holding the child, and saw heavy drapes at the windows suddenly curl away and become flames, a wall and ceiling of flames just in the time it took her to turn away to the door, to the hall beyond. Roger had the couple, pushing them. She followed down the hallway, the child quiet in her arms, wrapped in the blanket. She stumbled after Roger through the smoke, through flames that burned her face, down the stairs, stumbling, one flight, the turn, then another, then the third, the blanket over the child's face, and other arms now guiding her, faces in firemen's masks, into the arms of a massive fireman who said, "Jesus Christ, she's got a child!" and picked them both up and carried them outside into the air.

She held the baby tight until someone pried apart her arms and took it from her. A fireman shoved his own mouthpiece into Carrie's mouth and said, "Breathe!" She smelled her own burning hair.

They led her to an ambulance, past fire engines and wet, lunging firemen. She sat down on the step and let someone put a mask over her face, felt the cold stab of oxygen again. Her face was burning. Her chest was on fire, and she was wet. The air here was a half mist that began to cool her face. Her chest was still heaving and she thought of throwing up. Someone said, "Breathe slowly. Relax your muscles. Just relax." It was a medic, a young woman. The baby was inside, choking into an air mask.

"She's all right," the medic said. "She could have died in there."

Roger was beside her on the step. They took turns at the mask. MacKenzie was there, too, standing, his face black like Roger's but a clean space around his mouth, like minstrel faces. She laughed.

"You look like you're playing in the high school musical." She choked on the words but laughed anyway.

Roger was smiling. "We got everybody out, including us, and that's not bad."

The light was coming back to normal now, the flames drowned under tons of water. The young medic was swinging the doors closed. "Use the air over there." She pointed to the other ambulance. Then smiled at Carrie. "The baby's going to be all right. But I'd better take her in. I wouldn't lie. Have some more air. It's on the city."

The ambulance drove off, leaving an empty space at the curb, at the corner. Carrie reached for MacKenzie's arm. "Ian, I forgot. The red car. It was right there!"

She sat on the step, sucking air and taking away the mask to talk to them. The picture of the car was vivid.

"It was right there. Parked. The wheels were turned away from the curb. The tires were new. Big, new, black tires. They stood out like sore thumbs. Like Ward's or Sear's. New black tires on an old car."

She was starting to feel giddy, and a little silly. All that oxygen. She asked, "Roger, why did the light come on in that room?"

"I just flipped the switch. I couldn't see you. It was dumb, but it worked."

MacKenzie asked, "See the plates?"

"No. We were going full-out. And I wasn't looking for that damned red car."

"I've had enough bottled air," she told them.

She looked at the pair of them. Blue shirts blotched

with white ash and dark with wet. Faces blackened. Except for their mouths. She must look like that, too. A newspaper cameraman came up to them. "I got you coming down the stairs with that baby," he told Carrie. "I think I got all of you. But could you come back for one more, by the house, just to make sure?"

"Not back there," Carrie told him. "It isn't safe over there."

They walked to MacKenzie's car. Theirs was trapped inside the alley with the fire engines. MacKenzie said, "Take mine. I'll get a ride. I want to talk with the arson people."

They heard it on the radio, going in. Just parking at the station, in the lieutenant's slot. MacKenzie's voice.

"The fire appears to be the work of the Mission arsonist. Arson of opportunity, using rubbish in a side light well.

"There is a possible connection with the red, 1969, Ford LTD four-door sedan that has been sought in earlier sex crimes. All channels, please, headquarters. The driver is to be brought in for questioning by the arson detail.

"The car, headquarters, has new black tires. There are no other distinguishing characteristics."

They sat a while, just breathing. She said, "I can't take that in yet. Leong's car at our arson fire."

Roger said, "That's okay. It didn't take MacKenzie long. Rape and arson. Another of your old cops' tales."

Later, riding home with MacKenzie, Carrie said, "I'll never get this smell out of my hair. I hate it. I won't forget the dumb shock at hearing you on the radio channel, either. Putting it together. The fires, the rapes. I'm not sure yet what it means, but I suppose you do."

"I know the red car did the trick. Brighter minds than mine are working on that now. I don't feel all that sharp at the moment, but I will in the morning.

"For you and Roger, though, it's a day off. You've earned that. I'm signing you off sick, both of you. If your throats don't clear up right away, if your chest feels strange, check in at the police ward. Tell Roger, will you?"

"I'll call him."

She left him at his door. "I'll talk to you tomorrow," he said. "I expect to go downtown in the morning."

At home, she dropped her dark blue shirt and pants out on the small back porch and shut the door on them. And the shoes, those shoes. She shoved shoe trees into the wet mouths and shut them out in the fresh air, too. She stood at the sink and cut off the burned ends of hair. She'd get a real haircut tomorrow. Then she stood in the shower a long time.

She woke to the telephone. The chatty station keeper on the swing watch. She'd slept hours. "You're off sick, you and Roger. Your lieutenant dropped in to see my lieutenant. Have a nice weekend. But first read the evening paper. You're all over it."

She picked it up from the front porch and there she was, all over page one, in the middle. It looked like half the page. Carrying the little girl. Going down the steps, the child's face and hair just visible, firemen below holding out their arms for them. Her face was shining wet and black with smoke, and her hat was gone. Where was her hat? She didn't really care. She showered again to get the smell out of her nose, then went back to bed. Funny. She'd never thought she'd be in the newspaper, not like that. She was pleased. She guessed.

Roger called and woke her again an hour later. Wide awake now. He said, "They found your hat. MacKenzie sent someone back to look at the bottom of the stairs. He said he knew you had it on because your hair wasn't all burned off. Two hundred firemen stepped on it. They've got it in the squadroom now. It'll fit anybody."

Carrie said, "I'm ready to get up. I've just got time to pick up a new hat downtown, before the uniform shop closes, if we hurry. We can drop our uniforms at the cleaners. Have some dinner."

"That sounds good."

She said, "We could ask MacKenzie."

"He's busy. He spent the day downtown, then went

out to buy himself a new car. He said he just realized he doesn't have to have a station wagon anymore. After all those years. He could buy a Porsche."

"Oh, I forgot," she said. "Did he talk about the red car? Did they find it?"

"Not yet. Sex crimes said it's not conclusive. You've got your crimes mixed up. This was not a sexual assault."

"That house was raped," Carrie said.

"They said you didn't get the plates."

"Jesus!" She breathed it out.

"That's all right. Arson wants it. They're on the phone to Santa Rosa."

"Pick me up," Carrie said. "I'll be at the curb."

She picked through wet pockets and shoved the blues into a plastic bag. The shoes were still wet, too. She took out the trees and jammed newspapers inside, then rubbed oil in and oiled the soot off all her leather. Her gun needed cleaning, too, but not now. She wiped off the grit and locked everything away and was standing at the curb when Roger's brown Triumph turned the corner.

Before she went to bed, she talked to Spenser.

He said, "I've got the papers. The Santa Rosa paper has a different picture. It's very dramatic. They ran an old high school picture, too. Wanted to show you with a clean face, I guess. The year you won the two-hundred-meter down in San Diego. Also a picture of the trophy in the trophy case at the high school. I think that's all."

She said, "That was years ago. They had that in storage and then brought it out again for the press. It's embarrassing. I had long hair, too."

"I bought three of each."

"Good."

She settled down with a book, feeling clean again, hair cropped and clean. A lot less of it. Feeling rich. A day added to the calendar. MacKenzie called at midnight.

"Want to ride up with me in my new car? It'll mean you won't have your car up there."

"I can use Spenser's. It's grander. Sure. Anyway, he said he'd like to meet you. He said you were in the picture in the Santa Rosa paper. You were behind me on the stairs."

"I just went up to check," MacKenzie said.

"Okay. I'll be waiting. I could be working now. I feel fine."

"You earned a day, you and Roger."

She thought, What about you, MacKenzie? Lieutenants go on forever?

She hung up and thought, I didn't ask if he bought a Porsche.

She looked out at the dignified old tan Mercedes station wagon at the curb, MacKenzie standing there in slacks and cardigan. He looked pleased.

"It's as close to a sports car as I could get," he said. "I kept walking past it."

"I could get you a tweed cap."

He stood beside that lovely car and held the door open. Without his reading glasses his eyes had a twinkle. He shouldn't wear a cap, anyway, with that thick brown hair.

She walked around it and looked in at the old creased leather, new carpets on the floor.

"I sat in a lot of of sports cars," he said. "When you turn around, there's nothing there. You couldn't holler back at the children, or haul firewood or camping gear into the mountains."

She agreed. The car had a sense of purpose. She pictured him with his children. Holler, indeed. More likely he looked thoughtful and spoke softly and they kept quiet to listen, like his young subordinates.

He put her bag in back and she slid into the soft cushion of the seat.

He said, "I looked in all the showroom windows. The dealer had it sitting there with his new cars. I kept walking by, then going back again."

She settled her skirt and stretched out her legs. "If there were a reading light, I could bring a book for long night drives."

He grinned and pointed. "There."

She watched treetops gliding by. Then the cables and bridge towers, and small sailboats down below, a merchant vessel coming in. Then he began to talk. The taciturn MacKenzie.

"There's a long grade beyond Sacramento where you can look back in the mirror and see layers of haze covering the valley and the coastal hills, and you look up into the Sierra and you can almost taste the cold water in a mountain stream. See every rock.

"There's one curve where I always had to park the car and the kids would tumble down thirty feet to stick their heads in the cold water. After my wife died, I took them up a lot. Something about the country helped settle us all down, I think. I'm not sure what. They liked me to talk about growing up in those little towns, and knowing their mother when she was a girl.

"We married when I came back from the army. And children came, and I left college and went to work."

Carrie told him about her parents and of Spenser. Of the ritual of walking in the sand with him until they'd climb to the cliff's edge to sit and talk.

"That's where I decided to become a champion swimmer, and a schoolteacher and a police officer."

He asked what Spenser thought about her new career.

"I don't know what he actually thought but what he said was that it couldn't be more dangerous than teaching. At least I'd be armed."

Then they were both silent. The warm air washed over her. She closed her eyes for just a moment. When she looked at him again, he had his sweater off and they were driving past fenced rows of apple trees. He saw the look and smiled.

"I'll need directions from here on."

She guided him around the turn and past the hamburger stand, then onto the straight road to Forestville. The turn into the lane. Spenser stood there with young John. MacKenzie greeted the boy first, reaching down to shake his hand.

"I saw your picture in the paper, sir. You were rescuing Carrie from the fire."

"Not exactly," MacKenzie said. "She was the main rescuer."

Then John left, and the two tall men shook hands. Spenser seemed so slim, so gray beside MacKenzie.

They settled into chairs around the redwood table on the lawn, under the thin shade of the apple tree. Carrie brought out the pitcher of cold lemonade Spenser had ready. He also had the newspapers spread out on the table.

"You're a heroine in Santa Rosa," he said. "I hope you're up to that. Your old students will want to come to church on Sunday to see if you're there."

He told MacKenzie, "Her first schoolteaching job was here for two years, before she went into the city. There was a little story in our paper when she quit to become a police officer, but some of the more imaginative have suggested this was a cover for the Secret Service and God knows what else. Carrie suspects our local pastor. He's got his odd ways."

Carrie spread the papers out. "We get more space in Santa Rosa. Local girl makes good, I guess."

Spenser said, "They went back to interview the high school swimming coach about the day she swept the field in the two-hundred-meter down in San Diego, and another story on a term paper she once wrote on historic copper mines in the county.

"There it is." He pointed. " 'She Braved the Rattlesnakes.' "

"Bushwa," Carrie said. "You wear boots and carry a big stick."

"Actually," she told MacKenzie, "a lot of men mined copper around here but they dreamed of silver. Some old-timers still remembered stories about hidden silver mines.

"I had a good time doing that. Digging around in dusty old state files, and a whole summer following obscure old maps and trying to find landmarks that had been gone for years. I did find some old diggings. And some old people who remembered. There never was much copper, just a lot of hard work. But they had dreams."

She laughed. "And I wore out two would-be boyfriends. They went back to their souped-up cars and being big men at the drive-in."

Her eyes kept going back to the picture on page one. It showed her, hatless, the blond-haired child in her arms, a begrimed MacKenzie at her shoulder, just behind her on the stairs. He'd been there all along.

T hey became silent, shuffling through the papers. The countryside stretched out around them in bright sunlight. Carrie heard the mockingbirds rustling in the privet hedge, the babies fat now, running in the thicket, away from neighbors' cats. Jays were foraging noisily in the tall apple tree. It was nearly noon. The two men sat talking.

Her uncle folded his newspaper pages together, put them on the redwood picnic table. "They like to write of crime down in the city. Pillage and rape. It's an expression of local pride. It's somewhere else, not here.

"I find myself wishing now and then that could be true, but it's not. We may not lock our kitchen doors up here, but if we walled off our country village, I'm afraid the same crimes would be committed here inside the walls."

Carrie glanced up at MacKenzie. She said, "But it leads to this place. We've got a car that was near the fire, then disappeared. It was seen earlier near two of the rapes. We don't know where the car came from but the license plates were bought in Santa Rosa."

MacKenzie said, "We should have people there today and hope the press won't learn about it until we get it sorted out."

Spenser was concerned. "Rape and arson? Both?"

"It begins to look that way," MacKenzie said. "We can thank Carrie for putting that together.

"The car was first seen parked a short walk from two of the earlier rape scenes. Then Carrie spotted it when she and Roger were rounding a corner on their way to the fire. Until now, the men investigating the sex crimes have been doubtful. Now the arson detail is on the job. Perversely, they like the car."

"Where do you stand?" her uncle asked.

MacKenzie opened out his large square hands. "I see both sides. Two policewomen have claimed that some weeks afterward, one of them, who is gifted with instant recall, jotted down the car's description and license plate. A game they play, she and her partner. To list from memory a line of cars parked on a city street. Two crimes, two different dates. The car appeared on both her lists.

"Then Carrie thought she saw the car. They're calling it Carrie's car now. I can see an unattractive enmity toward women police officers in that. But that was the third sighting."

"All women?" Spenser's eyebrows rose.

"All three officers were women," MacKenzie said.

"So?"

"I believe them. I think we've got to find the car. But we walk with soft footsteps here in Santa Rosa. We have no evidence. No reason for a warrant. Even to ask questions. We do a dance step called the pussyfoot. See where it leads."

"It's not much," Spenser agreed.

MacKenzie smiled. "There's another level of pussyfooting going on. My own. This is no longer any of my business. But the sex crimes were once mine. I keep dropping by upstairs to look over shoulders. I keep my own crime map updated."

Spenser said, "You've got a daughter in Santa Rosa, Carrie tells me."

MacKenzie said, "There's also a captain in Santa Rosa. We go back a ways. I told him I'd drop in. Just for a chat. While the arson people are out looking for the car. Or the license plate, whichever we find first. We've got a confusion of two old cars and a single license plate."

MacKenzie glanced at Carrie. "I dropped in on another old friend last night in his office. He happens to be the chief. After I'd pulled a computer list of the fires and added them to my old map. Dropped it on his desk."

Carrie found herself reacting angrily to MacKenzie's grin.

"I won't breathe a word of this old-boy stuff," Carrie said. "I'd rather not even know about it."

Her uncle said, "I like maps. And I've never seen a police investigation at close-hand. Could I see yours?"

"Sure," MacKenzie said. "I brought it along to show my friend in Santa Rosa. So he knows what he's doing, unofficially. It's just an old street map. The kind I'd always do in cases where the suspect wasn't standing right there waiting to be handcuffed when we got to the door. It's in the car. I'll get it."

He walked through the grass to his car and pulled an ordinary street map out of the door pocket. Carrie helped her uncle clear away newspapers, iced tea glasses. Swept off the fallen apple leaves. MacKenzie unfolded his well-creased map and flattened it out across the table.

San Francisco. The Golden Gate Bridge at the top, and the broad bay. A piece of the Marin County shore. The Pacific Ocean at the left, the long green strip of the Golden Gate Park amid squares of city blocks. A row of four green crosses at irregular intervals along the top. Handwritten boxes of printed notes along the margin.

MacKenzie said, "The notes on four sex crimes. Starting with the dates, days of the week. As it turns out now, the dates are all-important.

"Three were on a Monday night, one on a Tuesday night.

"Other details. Ages of the victims, four in their sixties and seventies. The last one was twelve. Items taken. A shawl, a souvenir from Brighton, England. A gold locket shaped like a heart. A green cardigan, an embroidered handkerchief. Worthless souvenirs. Yet they may tell us something of the rapist, once we know more about him. If he saves them, they could link him to each crime. If we can find them.

"And, if you can read my writing, a note on each act of violence. He bit one woman's breast. Enough to draw blood. He bit another on the cheek, one in the throat.

"He bit the child hard on the ear. The surgeons will have a job repairing it.

"In her case, he didn't achieve his rape. She was too

young and vigorous. But he stood there and kicked her in the head, and in the back, with a heavy shoe or boot." Carrie straightened up from reading the small print. She watched the two men bent over the table, of a similar height but her uncle slim in his country khaki, MacKenzie a big tweedy man beside him. Their hands on the table, brushing at the fallen apple leaves.

"He is a vicious man," her uncle said. "He's filled with terrible feelings against the human race. But he takes it out on only the ones he can be sure of. The very old or the very young. How horrible to even think that he's still free."

His slim fingers traced more crosses in red ink across the lower part of the map, more blocks of neat printing.

MacKenzie brushed at them. "The fires," he said. "from the computer. Where they started. Here, in a light well. Here, underneath an old wood porch. Old houses, turned into apartments, some of them. The wood was old, ready to burn. He apparently picked up trash, old newspapers from the street, to set his fires. He carried ordinary kitchen matches.

"And the dates," MacKenzie said. "Days of the week. Each fire on a Monday night except one, on a Tuesday.

"You will note we have now filled in every other Monday-Tuesday combination from May 7 to September 17.

"And the car, the red car. Seen here and here and here. These red circles."

"It looks like a war map," Spenser said.

MacKenzie said, "Notes on the car. A 1969 red Ford with its distinctive shape. The tires black and new. The woman officer in the Taraval noted that. So did Carrie. New black tires on an old car at the curb.

"Intriguing but not enough to convince everyone. Last night we added a fourth sighting. Not by a woman or an officer this time. A man in the child's neighborhood who was not aware of what had happened to the girl, but went out for a walk and thought he saw a new brown car turn a corner.

"He looked at a red car last night under the new street-lights out there. It looked brown. He agrees, he could have seen a red car, not new but with new tires.

"Close enough," MacKenzie said. "That's the new red circle on the map.

"I woke up the chief to tell him. He's having new maps made today, by the professionals. With all this stuff. A real map this time. It should be ready by the time we get back into the city."

"Even your map is violent," her uncle said.

"The sex crimes people got our witness out of bed. So this one's theirs. Now both Sex Crimes and Arson have a stake in the red car."

"It stretches credulity to call that coincidence," Spenser said. "But I see your point. It's still not evidence. I wonder, though, how he arrives? Where does he go? Does he travel by the same routes each time?" His slim fingers brushing at MacKenzie's map.

MacKenzie pointed. "Major north-south thorough-fares parallel the beach. One-way streets lead right to them. He could arrive and leave again to the south, to the Peninsula, or turn north across the bridge. Enough traffic either way to mingle in. One more old car in the crowd. Even at that hour."

"The one-way streets run right at me," Carrie said. "So do the crimes. Look at them. They look like arrows.

And they're pointed right at my people in the Southern.

"I don't like that!" she said emphatically. "I don't like that one . . . little . . . bit!"

MacKenzie folded up his well-creased map. They all stretched and moved about in the warm grass.

"Your criminal," Spenser said. "You have no notes on him. On your war map."

"That's been difficult," MacKenzie said. "We have a composite drawing. We've put it out in the districts, but we haven't sent it any farther. We've asked the papers not to use it. We can't have a drawing the defense can use some day to prove we've arrested the wrong man. Given their ages, the violence, our victims aren't reliable.

"For instance, they all see him as a big man who towered over them, yet one woman, five-foot-four, said they looked at each other almost eye-to-eye. Before he hit her and knocked her down. He is short, therefore, for a grown man.

"Eyes. Not one of them can tell the color of his eyes." MacKenzie sighed. "They all agree he's young. That he wore a kind of suit or uniform. The pants and shirt apparently the same color and material. He wore heavy shoes or workboots. He had long blond hair.

"We know more about the car."

Spenser said, "He's a bully. You know that. I don't suppose it helps."

"Not much. Not now," MacKenzie said. "We've put out details on the crimes. His victims were three old women and a child. As you've said, he has a vicious streak. We'll wait and see if that triggers some cop's memory.

"Up to now, we've apparently got what every investigator hates—a new criminal. Nobody knows him.

106

"We have a blood type. A rapist leaves evidence of that. A few blond hairs. We don't know if he has AIDS. There's no HIV test for semen. A rape victim waits six months, then takes a test to see if her blood has the antibodies."

Spenser said, "The child wasn't raped, you said."

MacKenzie said, "She was bitten. Her odds are better but not certain. I'm sure the doctors will advise the family. In six months she'll take the test."

Carrie, watching the two men, listening, found it disturbing to hear words like this up here, amid these rows of apple trees, under these bright golden hills.

Her uncle said, "He's just part of the human race. There's nothing that stands out."

"No," MacKenzie said. "He's an aberration. He's always been a little different. Probably from childhood. Of all the millions of people on our coast, he's the only one we know of at this moment who's bent on this course of behavior.

"Once we find him, those who knew him, growing up, will say, 'Of course. I remember him. I knew there was something wrong with him.' So. We look for the red car. We want to see who drives it. Because right now, that's all we've got."

"I'm glad," her uncle said, "your life hasn't made you so cynical you see all of us like that. That you separate him from the rest of us."

MacKenzie smiled, but it was a sad, grim smile. Kicking at the bits of apple leaves the rampaging jays had torn loose to litter the grass.

"I have a firm belief there ought to be police around. In open view, in blue uniforms, where everyone can see them. Fleet-footed to chase down drug dealers and purse snatchers. We ought to be there to keep our fellow humans from snarling up the traffic. Or just hold back the crowds to let the parades march by.

"But we ought to be a presence that lets old ladies walk outside their own front doors at midnight. Or little girls take nighttime walks with the family dog.

"We must find this one, hold him up to public view to end his reign of terror, then lock him away. I don't know how long, perhaps forever. But we've got to find him."

Carrie gathered the young green beans, pitching the tough old ones missed in earlier pickings into a bucket for the compost, among the fallen apples. The Gravensteins that fell now in late summer plunged thirty feet and more from the topmost branches to thunder on the roof. Big and sweetly tart. With the bruises pared away, just right for applesauce and pies.

Spenser had been up before her, sauntering about in his old tans. Without looking particularly busy, he'd carefully rehung the kitchen screen door, awry from too many bangings, while she was putting bread in the oven.

A loaf for them, a loaf for Rosalee, and a loaf for Mr. Firthroe, who cared for their apple trees with his own, and harvested the apples.

Spenser was setting sprinklers on the lawn and flower beds when she climbed to the roof to collect apples. Anton La Pointe laughed at Spenser. "He could grease the tractor, that one, and not get his pants dirty."

John, if Rosalee could be believed, could stand idle in his room and his clean clothes would grow stains and tears. Of their own accord. Anton said in his precise English, flavored with the language of his childhood, "My son does not close the door. He throws it away."

She rinsed the beans in Spenser's fishing sink against the barn, and set the apples cooking on the outdoor burner, with salt and sugar and sticks of cinnamon and nutmeg and lemon rind.

The day's heat rose steadily. "It'll go all the way today," Spenser said.

"I'm going down to the creek before the coolness goes," she said. "Did you tell John about the club?"

"Oh, he'll come along. He likes tennis but he doesn't like so many girls. We've had some serious talks about how bothersome girls can be."

She laughed. "He's ten through and through."

Spenser said, "I suppose the phone will start again. The price of notoriety is having people who never liked you much come up and pat you on the back. We'll just let it ring. You're playing tennis?"

"Yes. I need it. And some long, hard swimming. We could do laps together."

"I can still swim," Spenser said. "And my tennis is good enough for John."

She picked up her book. "If the timer goes, will you turn off the applesauce?"

She left him there to putter.

The new pro played better tennis than she did but got nervous when she charged. MacKenzie, now. That made her smile. He'd just stand there and shove it back at her. But he wasn't built for tennis. He walked the mountains. With a pack and maybe a long stick, like his ancestors. She sat in the shade of a bay tree beside a stream that barely trickled this late in summer, and held an unread book.

They had dinner on the terrace of their restaurant above the Russian River, where white tablecloths glowed in the twilight and below them the broad brown dirty river was sunset pink. They wore cool cottons after a day of tennis and swimming in the sun. The owner and a succession of waitresses led them to their table. They were all Spenser's income tax customers, after all.

"John needs his own tennis racket," Spenser said. "Your old ones don't have any snap left. He can work it off in chores. I'll talk to Rosalee, so she won't think it's just another present.

"He plays like you," her uncle added. "It's time you had a game with him. When I feed him a soft serve, he steps up and bangs it past me, if he can. He won't just stand back there and wait for it."

Carrie laughed. She could see herself. Tall, gangling kid, burning with impatience. "Roger says would I please stop looking like I'm standing on my toes, ready to leap. It makes people nervous."

Spenser raised his eyebrows.

"I stand on the balls of my feet. Like Roger. I'm just there to sort out the good guys from the bad guys. I'm supposed to know the difference. Sometimes I do."

Nellie waited on them. She said everybody there had seen the pictures in the paper. She said it as if she didn't quite approve. "I knew women wore those uniforms but I never thought it would be someone like you."

Still, she brought cool plates of sliced and wedged fruit and vegetables and cold ham and chicken, and the sauces, and set out plates with her usual grace and a "There now" as she surveyed the table.

She asked, "You wear one of those guns? I couldn't tell by the picture."

"Yes, but I don't shoot it much. Just for practice."

Nellie made a small "Hmph" and went away.

"She comes from the age that reveres the teacher and the cop," Spenser said. "You're confusing treasured images."

Carrie said, "I should tell her I've got a sergeant who only cares about parades. She'd like that."

Spenser asked, "How about your old school friends? How do they react?"

"They take it in stride. Most of them. Some are a little envious. The uniform, the excitement. The women, mostly. The phys-ed history teacher is a bit standoffish, but he's always had his male dominance role mixed up. He acts like the playground cop. The kids manage to ignore him."

"Like blustering cops?" Spenser asked.

"Well, you ignore them. They frighten other people. They'd like to be like Roger, or MacKenzie, but they don't know how."

She described MacKenzie's redwood and glass home in the trees in the middle of the city, and told of smelling the fresh-mown grass at the Taraval station. "They keep a piece of old carpet at the door so people won't track the grass inside."

"And a bullet-proof grille to talk through if you want a quiet word with a policeman," Spenser said.

Carrie said, "And neighbors out with their trowels puttering in the station gardens. Don't ask me to sit here helping you to compound ironies. I'll end up with a sexy young Chinese cop whose mind photographs cars and license plates in a long string so that two months later she can write them down."

"Your red car. It's no wonder the police department can't believe it."

"It's not belief. It's what you do assuming she was right. You've got a license number and it leads to an older woman in the peaceful town of Santa Rosa and belongs to a gray Chevrolet she uses to shop and visit her sister in Berkeley. You don't have a red car at all."

"Except that you've got a red car," her uncle said. "It's been seen four times. You've seen it."

"I can still see it," Carrie said. "But I can't ask a judge for a warrant to roust an old lady who owns another car."

"Do you think your friend is right?"

"I think so. Even if I can't do it. Roger can, almost. He gets a stolen car every month. He says the plates flash at him as he goes by. But they don't flash at me."

"I've known minds like hers," Spenser said. "Such people can be useful. I have a different knack. Numbers tell a story. A long procession of them and the story unfolds, and when one number interrupts the narrative, it's wrong and I must stop and find out why. Hers tell a story, too. To her. But I don't know what I'd think if I were a judge, asked to sign a warrant. Except to ask for better evidence. Understanding your impatience all the while. You've seen the car."

"I can see it flashing by," Carrie said, "with new black Sears and Roebuck tires. It's almost malevolent. I can see his face. That drawing. It's all wrong. It's distorted by his victims. Eyes too large, ears wrong, chin wrong. They don't want to see his face again, even on a piece of paper. I wouldn't know him in a crowd but I think I'd feel him behind my back.

"It's like MacKenzie's map. That's the worst. The crimes march across it, west to east. They're like arrows, pointing right at me. Just where I don't want him. On my streets. I want to know how his mind works. Is he going farther and farther each time to commit his crimes? Driving up from the Peninsula or down from Santa Rosa, and making his escape going back again, under all our noses? Or is he frightened, going shorter and shorter distances?

"You answer me," she said, her eyes level. "Is he more

arrogant each time? Braver? Or is he a frightened man, committing each crime nearer home so he won't have so far to run?"

Her uncle's lean brown fingers circled the coffee cup. His white hair shone in the lamplight against the black night. As usual, he declined to be drawn into her intensity.

"I know why you don't see license plates," Spenser said. "You're watching all the people."

MacKenzie called when they got home.

"I'd forgotten how small babies are. They're calling her Agnes after my mother. Aggie. There's a red glint in her hair. I'm calling because I want to get back a day early. Get that map made."

"Good. Pick me up," Carrie said. "I need to repair all my gear."

She was ready when the tan station wagon pulled onto the gravel the next morning. On the road, she asked, "Anything at all on the car?"

He shook his head. "The Santa Rosa police went along to knock on the door but they didn't like it. They'd like a warrant. I can't blame them. From their point of view, it's pretty slim. They point out we could be wrong."

"Do you have any doubts?"

"She wrote it twice," MacKenzie said.

"I talked with the captain. We ran her operator's license on the computer, then her last name to look for a husband. She's the only one with that name in Santa Rosa. I'm not certain her license shows anything that helps us. She's just had one car since the system was put on computer, but she's lived in four different houses, one each in the four corners of town. The captain found that intriguing but didn't say why. She's been careful each time to give notice of a change of address.

"He'll tell his patrol sergeants. Put it down for passing calls. We'll see what kind of car pulls into the driveway. If it's a gray Chevrolet, that's the end of our string."

"We forget the red car?"

"No. We keep looking for the red car. We don't know the plates. We want to question the driver. Where he was at the time of the fire."

Carrie watched his face, relaxed, the firm lines softened. His attention was on the curving road, but she knew he felt her look. He had a slight smile. She said, "Spenser said you're a true Scot, implacable."

"It isn't just me," MacKenzie said. "Now we've got two bureaus working instead of one. Arson likes the car better than my old friends in Sex Crimes but everyone's got to pay attention to it now. And do their work. They're still knocking on doors. What else does your uncle say about the Scots?"

"Well, I got quite a lecture. He said they go off to be doctors and engineers, and work for the English, but always go home. Every hovel a castle, to be ruled and defended. They handle their women by giving firm orders on what must be done, then let them do as they please and take the position that was just what they wanted. Want more?"

"No. That's enough. That sounds like my mother and father."

On the freeway Carrie could feel the city approaching. "I'll drop you at home," MacKenzie said. "I want to go down and work out a new plan with Arson. I want to get

115

city trucks on at night. Get all cars alerted to call in piles of rubbish. Get it picked up before someone lights a fire with it."

Down the last grade to the bridge, the bay glinting at them like a blue mirror. Carrie said, "Sometimes going in I get the feeling all the bad guys are rested, too. They've had a long holiday and their energy is high and they're all waiting for me."

When she stepped out of the car, the heat struck her. Another heat wave was already upon them.

She and Roger took to the streets as a hot wind puffed through the narrow alleys, swirling dust and lifting newspapers and candy wrappers in a crazy dance. The city's wastepaper minuet. The sidewalks were hot and sticky and the city smelled and the wind was blowing the trash away.

"Blow it all to Oakland," Roger said. The wind made him edgy. It was Monday night. All their cars were on the street.

MacKenzie read aloud the alert for the red car, then

the scavenger schedules, the neighborhoods where side gates were left unlocked for the men who picked up the trash and set the night ringing with the clang of metal garbage cans. None in their sector. He read the captain's notice of his nominations for awards for meritorious conduct, hers and Roger's. Sent upstairs to the chief's desk. Maybe he would sign them. A bureaucratic gesture meant to encourage all police to rush into burning buildings. She said that to Roger. The wind sucked her words away and filled her mouth with grit. It would soon be inside her shirt and in her hair.

They parked in front of the old post office and walked north on Seventh Street. The first night after their long weekend. Ten workdays to go before another. A Monday and a Tuesday night. Nights of the weird crimes. Lights were on upstairs in the Hall of Justice where nine-to-five inspectors kept their coffee pots on Warm. They were patrolling, too. Sex Crimes and Arson plus specially assigned details in plain clothes. In department cars that looked like last year's Hertz models. Shirtsleeves tonight. They were on foot patrol, she and Roger. They looked at hands and faces. Everyone lived in the smell. Maybe it even smelled like this in Pacific Heights. Tonight.

"Maybe it's the last heat wave of the summer," Roger said. "Or next to last."

Her new hat felt stiff.

They saw four buses pulling in. One after another. Arriving all together from north, south and east. "Blue lemmings," Roger said. White faces looked out through blue glass windows at the city lights. She and Roger watched them file off, all ages, young and old, tugging at backpacks and sleeping bags. The old people had suitcases. Spilling out the doors of the bus station onto the sidewalk where street people eyed them.

She and Roger kept an eye out for young boys or girls by themselves, to stop them for a talk before the city swept them up and mixed them up to look like everybody else. Giving them addresses, YMCAs and YWCAs. Out along the sidewalks the runners from the Tenderloin were eyeing the newcomers for easy marks, prospective working girls or boys to be lured into a short walk and an interview with a man in mod clothes whose office was an El Dorado at the curb. None tonight. No tender ones at all tonight.

A scattering of migrant workers on the move. These stayed in the Southern. This was their neighborhood. While the money lasted, they had hotel rooms. Then they were street people. If they were still here in winter, maybe a friend would reveal the secret entrance to a warm burrow underneath the sidewalk.

She and Roger walked up to Market and watched the new crowd mix with the old along the block of bars and arcades, then turned back into the Southern.

"Why doesn't the wind ever clean the street?" Roger complained. "It just picks it up and puts it down again."

People shuffled past Carrie and Roger as they walked. No one looked at them. No one looked away. Some faces were familiar. The clothes all looked alike. Other people's clothes. The people went about their business, trading a dubious joint for a piece of stolen jewelry to be traded later for two quarters and a dime to make enough to buy the wine that would bring sleep.

Mixing with the revelers who spilled off Market and the dance of the arcades, the street people looked old and furtive. She and Roger turned toward Sixth Street. No trouble on the streets tonight. The pushing matches over wine or cigarettes would start in another hour but only feelings would get hurt. Like children on a playground. Without anyone to comfort losers.

The Market Street revelers usually stayed near the bright lights until it was time to catch a subway home across the bay or go looking for their cars, but tonight small clusters broke away to walk down Sixth Street toward the porno movie house. They grouped around the sidewalk boot and shoe emporium to buy cheap sandals. The distant loungers watched money changing hands, waited for the young crowd to walk away still pocketing change. The laughing crowd ignored the outstretched hands, clustered against the wind to roll cigarettes and light them, choking and laughing at the bitter taste as they walked bunched together down the street, leaving spilled tobacco and tobacco papers to blow away in the wind.

Behind them, farm workers off the bus were fingering the boots.

Carrie said, "If it's not shameful going to that movie, why do they look ashamed?"

"Next year it'll play the suburbs," Roger said. "They could wait and see it with their parents."

Street people had their dance, their way of meeting, pausing, almost touching in some ritual of exchange, then moving on. All their clothes came out of the same big box.

Once she'd made a protesting Alkron walk with her and Alkron said, "For God's sake, Lubick, they all fall down naked and sleep together and get up and put on one another's clothes!"

For warmth, Carrie thought. Alkron, you ought to know. That's what you do.

Roger looked at them as Carrie did. He didn't judge them. He watched and remembered faces.

They turned back along the alley, toward the radio car. A short patrol tonight. They'd need wheels on a weird Monday night. Their people were already bedding down along the walls or in doorways, on the hot concrete. Curled against the wind and grit, bottles held protected against chest and stomach, but loosely held in sleep. Some would lose their bottles before morning. Wrapped in brown blankets from the Salvation Army. In this heat.

She thought, Well, we're back, people. We've been on our weekend. Now we'll be with you for ten days.

In the car, they reported themselves available.

Roger pulled into traffic and they began their ritual of looking through open car windows, being looked at, going by.

In the Mission, other pairs of officers were searching out piles of combustibles blown into corners, calling in city trucks to pick it up. Extra cars were on patrol along the two crescents on MacKenzie's map, in the Mission, the Park, the Northern and the Richmond, police in plain clothes and in uniform. Looking for a red car. Looking for a man who walked alone. Pausing alongside any woman foolish enough to take her midnight stroll tonight on those quiet streets to suggest that daytime was better for a constitutional and tell her why.

Patrol cars were following the crash and bang and roar of the scavenger's trash crusher. Officers got out to relock the alley doors.

The four-car crossed paths with the two-car in the No Parking zone in front of the Harlequin Hotel. The city's reconstruction program had stripped away old buildings and left in their dingy places the new white structure with strips of green, floodlit lawn and doormen in pale lavender who kept the lawns free of street people but could only watch the patrol cars disapprovingly as men and women in gowns and black tuxedos left taxicabs at the hotel entrance after an evening of summer opera and late dinners. Getting off the streets. No longer a police problem.

Carrie nodded to Ed Wellington and Bill Massey in the two-car as Roger pulled back into the street, turning down past the gaunt red brick church with its dim floodlights, standing above empty parking lots where building rubble had been shoved into mounds by bulldozers, the brick and plaster dust tugged into white clouds by the gusting wind to swirl down the alley and settle on the lawns around the Harlequin Hotel.

MacKenzie called her in before the lineup. "They're moving the child to a private room," he said. "Hendry would like you to spell her for an hour while the child is sleeping. Actually, Hendry's got the room next door, but I think she'd like to go off and check her house, feed the cat. Can you start an hour early day after tomorrow? Stay two hours? Roger can start the watch on station relief, then you can join him. Just sit there and watch her through the window. If she's restless, go in and talk. Whatever it takes."

"Take notes?" she asked.

"Ask Hendry. She'll know what she needs. Put this down as overtime. An extra day's vacation. In some distant future."

He walked out to the rostrum and stood while they assembled. "Just pull up chairs," he said. "We'll keep it brief. The child is out of intensive care. Inspector Hendry said she's chatting up a storm. Wants to help the department artist draw a picture. Down to the buttons on his shirt.

"Pass the word. We'll save some phone calls. Just generally, we know our man is out there. We don't know where. We have some reason to investigate that red car. You know what it looks like. Stop any such car for investigation, identify the driver and notify headquarters. We will hold for questioning. That's all we can do. We don't have a warrant. No solo operations, please. Call for a backup."

"In the Southern, we'll have new crossing guards at intersections. They've had some training but they'll be nervous. Keep an eye out for any that need help.

"Meanwhile, we've got letters of commendation for Officers Henderson and Lubick, signed by the chief. They'll be invited to a commission meeting for their medals. The department's recompense for cleaning bills, and lost hair and eyebrows. And one regulation hat."

He glanced toward the bulletin board. "Which, I note, has been removed from the wall."

"I did it," Washoe mumbled. "I took it down to the department museum. They're friends of mine down there. I wrote a little blurb. 'This hat was stepped on by sixty-three firemen.' It looks it, too."

Carrie said, "I liked it where it was."

"It is enshrined," Washoe said. "Your name will go down in the annals."

Alkron said, "I know annals, George. I'll kick yours if you don't stop picking on my friends."

MacKenzie waved them on their way.

On the street, Washoe was still on his high. He blared out on the channel, "Hats will be worn. The first car to hear a foghorn gets a free cheeseburger at the diner."

"To divide? Washoe, your generosity is touching."

Headquarters intoned a bored admonition to keep the channel clear. The reply was a blast of classical music. The watch was settling in.

Carrie and Roger sat at the edge of the Hall of Justice parking lot, engine idling, radio on murmur. Assigned to simply wait. The wind was gusting now and then. Enough to rattle shop doors and set off the silent burglar alarms, send cars cruising by to "check the premise."

A tan car bumped over the grid into the lot and two men in sport coats climbed out and walked through the floodlights going to the door. McKitrick and Gallina. She'd heard them on the air. Big and little. Tough and sweet. The game they played. Criminals had games, too.

"Boy Four. At your convenience, check with the Two Hundred."

She acknowledged the call and climbed out. "I'll see what he's got."

MacKenzie had a large map spread out across his desk. No colored inks from random ballpoint pens. No creases and folds. It looked stark and businesslike.

MacKenzie said, "It's all here. We don't know where he goes or where he comes from. He can choose between two bridges. Go east or west. We might have missed him by no more than seconds. He might even have been seen. Just another old car. We'll post this in the districts with the bulletin on your red car. Next time we'll know."

Along the right-hand side was a neat paragraph on each rape, each fire, with the dates. They had started on May 7. Carrie had still been at the Academy. Cleaning up old teaching files. Driving old textbooks over to the used book store on campus. Long evenings with Spenser, aware of the crimes. She hadn't thought she might inherit them.

Now she was watching streets filled with victims, children and old women.

"McKitrick and Gallina said they have another witness. Someone out for a midnight walk. He saw a man bending over something at the curb, holding a kind of strap, wrapping it around his hand, then walking away. He didn't see a face, just that he was young. He's been away on business. He didn't know about the crime. Said there was nothing threatening about the scene, nothing that troubled him until neighbors told him. Then he called.

"He just walked in the house and went to bed. Said he didn't hear a thing. All that mess outside. He described the clothing. Gas station uniform, shirt and pants. Well starched and creased. He thought they were light blue."

Carrie said, "The child must have been lying there the whole time."

"Those lights again. Well, we know it was a uniform. We've got that, at least. The witness will think about it. They'll get back to him."

It wasn't much to know.

"What did he wrap around his hand?"

"Maybe a dog leash," MacKenzie said. "It's too late to call the parents. They'll do that in the morning. If it was, then he's got two new souvenirs, that and a gold, heart-shaped pendant he reached down and ripped off her neck. He can add those to the rest. I'd like to find the dresser drawer he keeps them in."

His face was grim, as it had been when he'd told about the dead child in the closet, then changed again as he saw Carrie was watching him. It was a constant face, normally composed and confident. How much of that was show, putting on a good face for the troops? Or maybe he didn't feel the irritations that so often moved her.

But he looked tired. Well, he'd been coming down here in the early mornings. When she looked again, he was smiling.

"It's all in train, as we say upstairs."

"I like trains." Roger's voice came through the door. "In fact, we have a date with a train. The engineer of the 4:02 wants to see an officer. Want to go wave at the engineer?"

They went out. Still no foghorns.

"All right, Carrie," she said to herself. "Settle in." Massey and Wellington were parked next to their car. Their turn for station relief. Sergeant McDowell was on the street. She said, "I'll drive it," and bumped out of the lot and into the turn to take them around to the Southern Pacific yards.

Carrie drove downtown that afternoon and parked in the Tenderloin a block down from the YMCA. She walked down the slight grade toward Market Street. The loungers, a mix of blacks and whites, eyed her aggressively. They owned the street and she was just a tall girl walking through in civilian clothes. The faces turned away as a Central Station patrol car cruised by, and as if someone had pushed a button, the people started moving up or down the street, crossed over, talked to one another. Busy. No loiterers on this block.

What could they have to do on a city block whose stores were empty, half the window glass papered over? Even the For Rent signs were dirty. She tapped at the glass door. No paper on these windows but they still weren't clean. Inside, the large, white-haired wife of the little tailor marched sternly across the empty room, looked at her and unlocked the door. The sentinel.

Inside, two long paper-covered tables at the back were littered with pieces of men's suits, cut and waiting to be sewn, and stacks of flimsy patterns. Odd saucers served as paperweights.

The tailor got up from his sewing machine, under a single bright light in the corner. He was the size of a child alongside his wife. Smiling, waving his hand at her uniform and blouses on a rack. His wife led Carrie back through a curtain into their kitchen dressing room, then marched back again to let her try on the clothes. She pulled on the pants. The damn things fit. Then the shirt. She walked out to let him dance around her.

"Put on the jacket, too! Try it on!" His little hands tugged at the material.

"Like a hunter!" he sang out. "Oh, I know about these things. Here, lift your arms. Way up!" He flapped his arms up and down and Carrie did the same. It all felt snug, but she could move in it.

He danced around her and sang out, "In Germany I make clothes for hunters! Just like this!" He'd made clothes in a concentration camp, MacKenzie said. And survived. This nice, foolish little man. He and his wife.

"I make hunting clothes like this, sometimes for women, too. The material is good! It will last and hold a shape."

"And get shiny," she told him, but he didn't notice.

She felt lighter. She did a pirouette before the single mirror, arms overhead, and saw two street loungers with their faces pressed against the dusty glass, watching in amazement as she turned in a dark blue uniform to reveal the shoulder patch, in gold, SFPD. The faces went away.

"Ah," the little tailor said. "You give me protection!"

His wife gave him protection, and MacKenzie's friends, the big men who came here to have their clothes fitted, jackets cut to hide a shoulder harness or waist gun.

"Is it all right? Does it feel all right? I like to do good work for all the police officers. If you want me to, some day I could make you a woman's suit of clothes!"

Another radio car went by outside. Forms went by the window, walking quickly. They kept them moving around here. In a block of empty storefronts.

She'd bring all her shirts, she decided, and her other uniform. The tailor's wife draped her new clothes over her left arm, handed Carrie her purse, eyebrows raised at the weight of the gun. Opened the door. Kept it open as Carrie started down the street.

Well, now her clothes fit. Maybe she did, too.

That night she felt almost trim. No bunches of material between her legs. Her shirttail stayed where it belonged. She moved around the locker room with pleasure, shoved a fresh battery in her radio, clipped the mike at her shoulder, pushed the button. Walked past to check the bulletin board, working at her new hat to get the stiffness out. MacKenzie was in his glass cubicle, on the telephone. Taking notes. When he came out he just waved at them. The chatting stopped. He said, "I just heard from Santa Rosa."

He looked pleased. "Our car is there. Officer Lubick's red car is parked at this moment in the driveway of a private home. It's got our plates. We don't have a driver. There's some confusion in the registration, but we've got our car. The owner is an older woman who claims she is the only one who drives it. She can't locate the registration papers but she owns it. The Santa Rosa police will make a formal report for the people upstairs, who can then respond with a formal request that she be questioned more extensively." He smiled. "Thus we preserve the paper trail.

"She's been handed a citation for an infraction involving registration. That may give a little leverage, not much, but at least we have a red car as described by two officers in the Taraval and one Southern Station officer who saw it at an arson fire."

Everyone in the room was grinning.

MacKenzie said, "I may tell them upstairs, before the paper gets there."

They all laughed. They knew the bureaus.

Well, Carrie thought, looking around the room, some people believed she'd seen a car.

Washoe said, "Sacramento probably got the registration screwed up. They always do."

MacKenzie said. "Not this time. She said the plates were hers. She paid for them. She just took them off her old Chevy and put them on the red Ford."

Lawrence Kang said, "That's what I do. My wife says it's all right."

MacKenzie said, "She said her son did that. But he doesn't live with her. He doesn't drive her car. They handed her the citation and she said she'd call her lawyer. Closed the door."

"Jesus, lawyers!" said Ed Wellington.

MacKenzie was smiling.

"You see, Officer Lubick. It all comes together."

He said, "I'll find Sergeant McDowell. He's got today's teletypes. Then I'll pay a visit upstairs."

"Let 'em eat crow," Washoe said. "It'll be good for 'em." Alkron punched him in his beefy shoulder. "Well," he said. "I knew there was a car."

Carrie and Roger pulled out the rear seat of their car for the usual check for guns and knives missed in a lazy pat search. (Smart prisoners always said, "I never saw that before. It's not mine.") Rammed it back. Others were checking their cars. In the distance, beyond the clamor of the freeway they heard something. Roger held up a hand for silence and they all paused to listen. Faint but distinct, they heard the two-tone baying of a foghorn, then again, a different note, as one talked to another up the bay, marking the slow drift of the incoming fog. There was a scattered cheer.

The fog bank moved in a cold mass that would sweep along the broad avenues and around the city's hills, slip between tall buildings and into the narrow alleys of the Southern. She shivered in anticipation.

"I've got new pants. I can run without holding them up. Let's do hotels."

The air had cooled, but the heat and the odors still lingered in the buildings. They had started at the Market end of Sixth Street, pushed through the first heavy wooden door with its faded and chipped gilt lettering across the windowpane: HOTEL EXCELSIOR. They pounded up the narrow stairs.

Their heavy shoes were kettledrums muted only by worn carpeting and their gear rattled going up. They turned off into a hallway fitted with a four-foot desk, an East Indian woman in a sari sitting on a stool. She pushed the hotel register around for Roger to see, watching his face with somber eyes. She was thirty, with a husband and children somewhere in the hotel. An official city notice under a plastic cover prohibited cooking in the hotel rooms.

"Whew!" Roger breathed out. The small lobby, like the corridors, smelled of old curry and garlic. A couch with green plastic upholstery against one wall, an old stand-up hotel ashtray beside it. A leaning bookshelf with schoolbooks. She saw a third grade reader, sixth grade arithmetic. Binder notebooks stuffed with papers. Roger pushed the register back, said "Thank you." No boxes here marked with the room numbers. No one left messages for tenants in the hotels of the Southern. A row of pegs on the wall behind her, no keys on them. "We are full tonight," the woman said in precise English. "The farm workers have come in."

A narrow band of colorless carpeting stretched away on either side down narrow corridors, a faint flower pattern at the edges. Wooden doors with chipped paint. Some of the dime store imitation brass room numbers were missing. At one end of a corridor, she felt the thumping of a jukebox from the bar downstairs. She could feel it in the floor.

She and Roger once had a knifing victim in one of the top rooms here. They'd waited in the hall until the sergeant came, then the crime lab and the coroners, homicide inspectors in three-piece suits. A heavy man face down on the bed, a wet stab wound in his back. Old jeans. Worn boots on the floor. His feet were bare. That was the saddest sight, those naked old scarred feet. Whiskey bottle near his crumpled hand, its cap twisted on; a wallet. A wet puddle of blood on the blanket but no knife. Maybe in the bedclothes. Probably not. Good knives cost money. "This time we got here before the flies," Roger said.

Mrs. Patel had not seen anyone arrive or leave. The coroner's men were quickly in and out. Carrie made notes in her notebook, then handed the man from Homicide the green card from the wallet. A Mexican farm worker. Now he couldn't send his money home. None left to send. Juan Gomez. Like Patel, a common name.

Roger said to the man from Homicide, "Your perpetrator isn't one of ours."

"Oh?" Cool disbelieving eyes.

"There's some whiskey in the bottle."

Perhaps there'd been a woman. Mrs. Patel shrugged. She couldn't say.

That had been a long night. Roger had said outside, "Well, you didn't throw up."

"Thanks, Roger."

"You'd be surprised. The tough ones always do. The hard part is the sadness. The ineffable sadness. It's part of your new life, if this is what you want to do."

Tonight they jangled up another flight and walked the halls.

The next hotel had a cardboard sign. The Hotel Baron had changed its name to Seadrift Inn. The carpets had once been green. The plastic couch was red. The man behind the desk, also an East Indian, pushed the register around.

The smells, the day's leftover heat, were the same. The cooling fog didn't creep in here in summer. In winter, Carrie knew, these walls would be cold and damp. There were a few keys on their pegs. The late drinkers. The bar music downstairs thumped through the floors.

On the street a prostitute from across Market was screaming at them. Her skimpy clothes were awry. "He stole my money! That one, there he goes! In the red shirt!"

She pointed at a crowd of farm workers milling around on the sidewalk down the street, standing, talking. Going in and out of bars. Every fifth one wore a red shirt.

"No he didn't," Roger said. "She gets her money first. Before she says hello. He punched her in the eye. Her pimp's going to do it again if she can't work."

No, she didn't want the hospital. She didn't want to file a report. "All right," Roger said. "If we find this Jose, we'll come across Market Street and look for you. What's your name?" His pencil on the page of his notebook.

"Shit! You're all alike!" One eye swollen almost shut. She turned back toward Market Street, pulling her short skirt straight over a skinny bottom. Her walk became a high-heeled strut in scuffed orange shoes that flopped on her feet. They'd once been someone else's.

"Let's drive," Carrie said. "Everything is sad tonight."

"You drive it," Roger said. "I'll trust you."

Carrie twisted the car slowly through the alleys. Older men and women were coming home from late night work. She drove past the small opening she once walked through, a row of shirts still on the clotheslines overhead.

They were the late car. They would be here in the morning when the streets became a bedlam of traffic jams and honking horns, children waiting at the intersections for the white-haired crossing guards, some of them with long black hair down the backs of summer dresses.

At a soft run, Carrie moved through puddles of light under the streetlights, past the neat lawns and privet hedges of her neighborhood, her body growing moist inside the running suit. Then she reached the hard beach sand and pounded along at the edge of the dark ocean and white surf, stretching out. Then turned to work her way back through the soft sand to the macadam of the neighborhood streets, still soft from the hot sun of afternoon.

The tan Hertz car pulled up from behind pacing her and she looked over at Leong smiling through the open window.

"Hi," Leong said. "We're out warning potential victims off the streets until all the bad people are in jail. It's amazing how many respectable women like to walk at night."

Carrie slowed to a reluctant stop.

"We're promoted to the robbery car. In consideration of our great coup with that old car. It's just temporary."

They looked like two high school girls who'd stolen a police car and blue uniforms.

Kedrick leaned around to ask, "You do this all the time?"

"Just warming up."

"We come in early and stay late," Leong said. "Your lieutenant came out for another talk. He didn't just pick up the phone. Sergeant Poggi said they're taking our car seriously. I guess we're real."

"Temporarily," Carrie agreed. "I'm getting cold. I've got to go."

Driving in through the neighborhoods she kept crossing paths with black-and-whites. It looked like maneuvers, as if all the cars in the department were weaving around these streets.

She fitted her small car into a police slot beside an ambulance and walked through antiseptic corridors. A nurse pointed to the elevator. A chair stood outside the girl's room. She saw Inspector Hendry through the window. Carrie waited until the gray-haired inspector noticed her and tucked her knitting into a bag at her feet, stepped through the door and closed it softly.

"There's not much to do. She likes to chat at odd hours. If she wakes up, go in and sit with her. She's just now getting used to sleeping nights. They've done a lot of pushing her around."

Good, level eyes, gray as her hair. She wasn't as tall as

Carrie. She smiled. "I'm glad you're in uniform. Sometimes she doesn't believe I'm a police officer."

"What should I avoid, if she wants to talk?"

Hendry looked surprised. "Nothing," she said. "Don't pussyfoot. She's too smart for that. You'll find her very forthright. Talk about anything she likes. If it's something new she's just remembered, she'll tell you. Take a note. Leave it for me in the drawer. She'll show you."

As if Carrie still looked doubtful, Hendry said, "Look, she won't break. She's a blunt and honest child, maybe a bit like you."

Hendry laughed at her surprise. "Oh, I watch all of you come and go. With my gray hair nobody sees me looking. I think you'll do. I asked Ian to send you over. Now let me go and get my house in order. I've got to get some pretty lavender yarn I've been saving. I'm making her a sweater. Sleeveless, so she can swing her arms around. She throws a lot of basketballs in her school clothes." A ghost beckoned to Carrie out of her own childhood.

"See you in two hours. Then I'll get some sleep. My notes for the detail are in the drawer. Take them with you when you go. You can read them, if you like."

Carrie tiptoed in. Brown hair on the pillow, not as dark as her own but cut short like hers. A white bandage covering one ear. No monitors but an IV connection on one arm. Slight form in the bed, chest rising and falling evenly.

Carrie was surprised at the thought that she was watching herself as a child in that bed. She could almost hear the cries of her old neighborhood through the unopened window, but listening, heard only the drumming of the freeway a block away, a clinking sound far down a corridor, someone carrying a tray. The face turned away on the pillow was the lovely face of another child.

Two curious brown eyes gazed at Carrie.

"Don't be startled," the child said. "I've got used to waking up and seeing new faces. It doesn't bother me."

"Do you need something? Hurt anywhere?" Carrie asked.

"She said she'd send a real police officer," the child said. "So she did. The answers are no, and yes. I hurt all over, but I always do these days. I could wiggle around and test the sore spots but I'd rather not. I perspire, then I'm in my own warm puddle. If I don't move, it won't hurt. For a while."

The face on the pillow smiled back at Carrie.

"Talking hurts a little. Smiling does. It pulls my ear, you know. Where he bit. They're going to put it back together surgically. Good as new. I doubt that, but they try. They're reassuring but not always honest."

Carrie said, "I was told to take my kid gloves off. Now I see why. I don't wear them very often, anyway."

"Good. She said she'd send someone I'd like. She has to go home and feed the cats. Does she really have cats? Or is that another euphemism?" The child was speaking carefully, holding her head still on the pillow. Her eyes were appraising but friendly, and still curious.

"I'm Elizabeth," she went on, "and I like that better than Liz. Beth would be all right but it's old-fashioned. Like Good Queen Bess. What's your name?"

"Carrie. Short for Caroline. My mother called me Caroline when she got impatient, so I never liked it. Short name, short hair. It fits under a police hat and dries fast after swimming."

"Good," the child said. "Maybe, if we get to know each other, we'll be friends."

Carrie said, "I have one friend your age. I could keep track of two."

She thought, I like this child.

"I don't get frightened lying here. You ought to know that," Elizabeth told her. "If I want my medicine, I can ring. I've got a button tied to my left arm. I have to move my arm to show you, though, and I don't want to. It's all going to hurt awhile. At least I'm still a virgin.

"The therapist says I'm a virgin until I give consent. Do you go along with that?"

Carrie was still pondering when Elizabeth said, "That's all right. Inspector Hendry doesn't either. What happens, happens. It's just something that happens to your body. Like getting hit in the nose with a baseball bat. You've got a broken nose. It gets better.

"Mostly I got knocked down and kicked."

Carrie nodded. "I read the reports. I know a little."

"About Trixie, too? Dumb name for a dog, but I was pretty young. I'd have given her a proper name if I'd been older. We just went out for a walk, you know. She liked to walk at night. When I think about it, that's the bad part. Thinking about going out my own front door again. I'll be afraid when I do that at night and that makes me mad. It's my own door!

"I could have ducked back inside, you know. Except for Trixie. She wanted to fight him right away. I guess she knew he was weird. So I was trapped. I didn't like that part. I couldn't go back in and I couldn't run away. You know, she fought him off, and I did, and I kept hollering. I punched him off and she was biting him and that's when he bit my ear. That really hurt!

"Then he kicked me and the lights went out. They did really, you know. I couldn't see anything. But I heard him. Kicking something else. I knew it wasn't me. I knew who he was kicking. That's what I won't forgive him for! Not as long as I live!"

It was a lovely, round-cheeked face, pale now but with a scattering of freckles high on her cheekbones, and those brown steady eyes. Carrie was beginning to know victims. They wore an air of guilt. As if it were their fault. Not Elizabeth.

"The therapist says it's all right to talk about it. Actually, I don't mind. Some of it bothers me. Hendry says if I talk about it long enough I'll get bored with the whole thing.

"But I keep remembering new bits. I want to see his face very clearly. I'm going to describe him to a man named John Carruthers, the Police Department artist. You must know him. We're going to do a picture.

"Some day I'll get on the witness stand and say, 'That's the man, right there. I know because he's got that little scar under his right eye. And his eyes are green. I saw that before the damned door slammed shut behind me. And he's got that hurt little boy look on his face, like he's angry and he's going to cry. Bullies get that way at school when you hit them. Then they run away. Like he did.' "

Carrie put a hand out, touched a shoulder. "If you get worked up, you'll lose your puddle."

Elizabeth smiled back. "No I won't. I was thinking, It would be nice if you could catch him, but I don't suppose you will. The detectives will do that."

"Probably," Carrie said. "That's what they do."

"I'm not always such a chatterbox, you know. I might just drift off to sleep again. It's all this painkiller. Will you be here?"

"Or Inspector Hendry will. One of us."

That smile again. Then the eyes were closed, but she was still chatting. "I should have said I liked your uniform. I'm not certain I'd be suited to be a police officer. I still think I'll be an anthropologist. I can make big pictures out of little things. You know. Of course, I don't have to decide just yet."

She was asleep. Carrie watched. No ghosts. A real child. Already mending.

Inspector Hendry's notes were neatly written:

No typewriter here. Someone will have to enter this in the computer. Elizabeth and I worked out his height. Her eyes were at the level of his Adam's apple before he first made a grab for her. She'd just come off the top step and was shouting at him to leave the dog alone. He's 5 foot 6.

The eyes are green. She saw that before the door shut behind her, since there is a question about the effects of the streetlights there. And the faint scar with a half-moon shape under his right eye, one quarter inch in length. I described this earlier for the teletype. His gas station uniform was gray, heavily starched and sharply creased. Right out of a commercial laundry.

The shoes as she described them sound like hightop workboots made with unfinished leather. They are important because they are splotched with different-colored blobs of paint. She saw his boots while she lay on the ground and he stood above her. We may be looking for a man who works in a paint shop. When he is found, his footwear should be tagged for evidence.

The dog leash. The new witness says he took it with him. He also ripped a gold heart-shaped pendant and gold chain off her neck. This will make good corroborative evidence, if we ever find it.

The leash is sold in pet stores for a medium-size dog, perhaps five feet in length, tan leather. It was new at Christmas so is not badly worn. It is ornamented with a red glass "jewel" set in brass every eight inches. The second one is loose in its setting. The fifth one has been replaced by a blue jewel, and the brass is scratched where she bent it back with pliers. The jewel nearest the dog's collar is missing altogether.

Her parents can identify the pendant. There are family snapshots in which it shows clearly, I am told. The child can identify the dog leash. She bought it out of her allowance.

Carrie took the notes to the records room for the computer. Phoned the sex crimes detail to watch for it in half an hour. Things to add to a new Teletype. Pulled a fresh battery out of the charger box. She waited for Roger at the door, by the bulletin board. The new watch named the new officers assigned to the Southern, from the Academy or other district stations. She didn't know them. Alkron was riding with Bill Massey from the Northern. Washoe had a new partner.

The captain was meeting with people from the Vietnamese and Laotian communities to discuss their problems with security. The high-rise for seniors had beefed up security. A retired police inspector was in charge. Temperatures, day and night, had dropped fifteen degrees.

Roger was standing by their car. "I had it washed so they can tell us from the taxicabs. We're full of gas. Washoe's got some blonde with him, covering our sector. Alkron looked her over good. She can tell you what she's wearing underneath. Down to the color of the polish on her toenails, if you care to know."

"I don't care."

They checked in with headquarters. Washoe in the two-car to the west, Alkron and Bill Massey in the three-car on the waterfront. Carrie drove a pattern through the alleys, then past the boot stand and the Greyhound. The five-car had a motel robbery. The windows were all closed tonight along the alleys. There was a bustle on the air. The fog was in.

"What's she like? The kid?"

"Her name is Elizabeth. She'll never make a good victim. She just met another playground bully. A larger version. I'm sure it goes deeper than that but I think she'll be all right. One thing, we'd better get this guy before she does. She has a fine anger about that dog.

"Another thing, I like Hendry. That's a good, wise woman. I could learn from her."

After the first hour, Roger took the wheel. They straightened out a small beef with farm workers near the Greyhound. Some slicker from the Tenderloin was peddling tickets in a lottery, which were now strewn along the alley. No blood, no injuries. Carrie stood there while they sorted themselves out.

"A little private enterprise," Roger said.

MacKenzie found them between warehouses and pulled his car onto the sidewalk for a talk. They switched off the engines. Radios at murmur.

"We've got a name," MacKenzie told them. He sat at the wheel three feet from her. Roger leaned across to listen.

"They've talked to residents around all her former homes. Apparently this woman moves a lot. They've traced the son back to childhood. His last name is different. She was divorced and remarried, or took her maiden name.

"Old neighbors described him as a loner, an unpleasant child. One said he played with her children, went to the same schools. The mother didn't like him. Said he was a biter. She had to tell his mother.

"She said the boy's mother thrashed it out of him with a leather belt."

They sat silently over that one.

"That's the game some parents play," Roger said. "Pass it on."

"Sacramento says he has no operator's license. Never had one. If he's ours, he drives a car but he's never been pulled over, not even as a teenager."

"An oddball," Roger said. "Every sixteen-year-old gets a license. And gets tickets."

MacKenzie nodded. "My friend the captain has a good estimate of his age. At some point, he didn't move into a new apartment when his mother did. The detail has been checking nearby counties for a phone number. So far he has no phone.

"Tomorrow they'll shake up the local school principals, get someone to go through old school records."

"Then what?" Roger asked.

"We'll have a date of birth, perhaps a blood group to match against the one we've got."

MacKenzie said, "The new Teletype is out. It's got the facial scar, his workboots. Now his name is on it."

Later she passed McKitrick and Gallina with MacKenzie in his cubicle. They even nodded to her.

She drove MacKenzie home. "They've traced him to his high school. Then it got too late to catch people at their desks."

"We're closer, aren't we?"

He nodded.

"He could be the one."

"We're looking for a troubled man," MacKenzie said. "This one could be ours."

"You'd like that child," Carrie said. "I'm glad I'll be seeing her again. I'm surprised at the violence of my feelings. I think now I understand that rule about not letting someone bring a rapist in alone. It ought to include female officers."

"It does," MacKenzie said.

She dropped him at the redwood house. Another night had slipped into foggy day.

Her days were starting differently. Again she walked down a hospital corridor to join Hendry just outside the door. Elizabeth was sleeping, head turned away on the thin pillow. Hendry's knitting bag was on the floor beside the chair, a patch of lavender showing. "We're into the new purples," Hendry said. "My granddaughter will get blue. Maybe she won't mind. She's only three." She laughed. "Or maybe I'll have to lay in a stock of purples. I wouldn't be surprised. Three can be most decisive. She was through with pink when she turned two."

Carrie said, "There are radio cars running around all over the city. We must have borrowed some from Oakland. All the cops inside are busy looking out the windows. They look either mad or bored, but they're awake. That will surprise the citizens. The trouble is, they don't know who they're looking for."

"We'll have a drawing soon," Hendry said. "I think she's almost ready." She laughed. "She wants to start right now! She's good for twenty minutes, then falls asleep again. You had a taste of that."

"When can they do it?" Carrie asked.

"When the doctors approve. Then her parents must say yes, and the therapist. Elizabeth does the pushing. I don't have to. Well, I'm off. You can just sit out here unless she wakes up."

It wasn't long after she'd settled into the chair that she saw movement in the room, Elizabeth turning in her bed, looking at Carrie through the window. She went in.

Her face was moist. Carrie found cool water in a bowl, wrung out a washcloth and wiped her brow and cheeks.

Elizabeth said, "I dream a lot. Sometimes I go through that wrestling match again. I don't always win but I'm not sure what happens when I lose. I didn't know what he wanted. But I knew. I kept saying to myself, 'I don't believe this idiot. Why me? I'm just a kid.' Then I wake up."

"You had bad luck," Carrie said. "Odds are you won't again."

"I was mad at him. When I get in this weepy mood I think maybe that's what did it. If I hadn't been mad, he might have walked away."

"No," Carrie said. "You didn't do it. It was all inside his head. He didn't care what was in yours."

"Maybe he never had a dog that someone kicked," the child said. "Then he'd know."

Carrie sat in the chair and kept her hand near Elizabeth's hand on the counterpane. There for touching.

"When I wake up feeling good," Elizabeth said brightly, "it's because I've been dreaming of my new school or something. I have new clothes to wear, you know. It's a girls' school and that's sort of yucky but there's a boys' school down the street and we have the same playground. Do you know my school?"

"I used to be a teacher at the public school a few blocks away."

"That's funny. You look so natural in your uniform. I'll have to think about you being a teacher."

Carrie said, "It's almost the same. The people are bigger, that's all."

"Our playground supervisor had a whistle," Elizabeth said. "I have a video of an old movie where a policeman blows his whistle all the time and everybody runs around. It's pretty silly."

She paused. Carrie felt the warmth of the other hand.

"I'll be late starting school," Elizabeth said. "So everyone will notice me. I'll probably have this dumb bandage on my ear. They'll all ask what it's for. I've been making up things to tell them. I just want to go to school and make friends, and play on the playground and beat up on boys my own age. You know. I don't want to be peculiar."

Tears started in her eyes and ran down her cheek. Carrie reached out and brushed them away.

Three new seven-to-three watches were in place tonight. Roger was the leader, with a new sergeant out of the Academy. Carrie had a new partner, Lawrence Kang, whom she knew. He'd been riding with Ed Wellington. His wife dropped him off in a new Volkswagen Golf. She had a shop in Ghirardelli Square. It was Sunday. They were beefed up and waiting a day ahead of the anniversary of the crimes along MacKenzie's crescent.

Kang was waiting in the parking lot, as tall as she but broader. She handed him the sheets of stolen cars. "I'll drive. It's my neighborhood."

"You pull a foot patrol, you and Roger."

"When we can. When we have time. It all changes. The farm workers were in town last night. We'll see if they're still here. Maybe we won't have any street fights tonight."

Wellington called in a body under the bridge approach. She parked behind the other radio car. "I'll go up," she told Kang. "You can keep the cars from getting stolen."

She used the flashlight to step through piles of windblown trash. Wellington's light was blinking up ahead underneath the concrete arms of the bridge. Nobody ever came up here. There weren't even any sayings from Mao spray-painted on the concrete. Wellington had his back to a slight form in old cords and jacket on the ground. A woman, partly on her back with her legs pulled up into her stomach.

"I looked at her once," Wellington said. "You can't tell which one is hers." He flashed his light at the bottles littering the ground. "I thought she was winking at me," he said. "You don't have to look. I have to write it." His new partner was off examining some piles of trash twenty yards away.

Carrie flashed her light at the emaciated form. Thirty going on sixty. Her eyes were open. When the headlights of a car flashed by, she winked. But she had no eyes, Carrie saw. They were maggots.

"I didn't sign on for this," Wellington said.

She saw the coroner's wagon pull in below, flashlights coming up the hill. She passed them going down. "You'll have to carry her," she said.

"It's a woman?"

"One of ours," Carrie said. "She used to sit with her friends along the wall on Fifth Street, passing a wine bottle. I don't suppose any of them know her name."

She went down the hill. Roger's words. "The sadness of it."

They got back in their car and she began the slow zigzag through her alleys.

Kang said, "My father is amazed that I work here. Where we used to live. When my parents first came over." He pointed at one of the thin Victorians. "It was like that one. I was two when we moved out to the avenues. All I remember is the back porch in the sunshine, so I guess it was on the south side of the alley. He pretends he can't remember the address."

Kang liked patrol. He stayed alert, lifted a friendly hand to the nighttime workers coming home along the alleys. The cooks and janitors, cleaning people in the high-rise offices. They were sent into the Central to help straighten out a bunch of Indians struggling halfheartedly with a group of blacks in the Tenderloin. Kang got out. He was big enough to separate them. "They're too drunk to hurt anyone." He waved the Indians back toward Market Street.

"The Indians are ours," he told the two cops from the Central. "Send them all back to the Southern. We'll watch over 'em."

"My father likes my uniform," Kang said. "That's power and respect in Korea. He'd like to see me wearing captain's bars, live in a better neighborhood. He'd think all his hard work was worth it."

"What work did he do?" Carrie asked.

"Does," Kang corrected her. "At home he was a barrister. Here, he got a job with a strong union. He's a janitor. Once he went on strike. He walked a picket line and nobody even shot at him. The cops didn't beat him up and throw him in jail. He's got more power here than he did in Korea."

They drove around their warehouses. The chatter on the radio ran down toward dawn. It was Monday.

She would have Kang with her through Monday and Tuesday night, MacKenzie said. Roger would work the residential areas they were concentrating on. As usual, what concerned her most was happening somewhere else. Nobody really thought that crazy man would wind up in the Southern.

"We don't even know what he looks like," Kang said. "You can't see green eyes or a scar out a car window."

On lower Market, she saw three forms huddled against one of the concrete sidewalk barriers outside the subway. Carrie got out to find a man and woman in their thirties, nice-looking, holding one another, a five-year-old boy squeezed between them. Two old suitcases were beside them on the sidewalk. They looked back at her with mute eyes.

"We hitchhiked from Minnesota," the man said. "They told us there was work. We came over on the subway."

"I'll need your names," Carrie said. "Make a report. "We'll send someone to pick you up. You can't stay here with that child. There's a church just up the street. They've got some cots. We'll get you a ride."

She found two ten-dollar bills in her wallet and folded them carefully into the woman's hand. When she told Kang, he got out of the car, too. Took some bills out of his wallet.

"It won't pay a first and last month's rent," Kang said. "You can't be out of work in Minnesota, in the farm country."

She told MacKenzie later, "I've got a child who wins when she's awake but loses in her nightmares, and a body under the bridge that used to be a woman who told funny stories and drank wine with her buddies, and a nice couple who came out here because someone lost a farm in Minnesota. They shouldn't be sitting on a sidewalk! They should be in a house!"

MacKenzie looked away. "We're doing something awfully wrong," he agreed sadly.

Then he said, "But until somebody figures it all out, we'll be the ones to clean it up. At least you had a church to call. Fill out one of those new forms for the mayor."

He didn't need a ride tonight. He had his car.

"I'll see you tomorrow," she told Kang. "I think I'll take a little run."

"If the patrols out there will let you," Kang said. "They're bullying everybody off the streets."

Elizabeth slept amid a scattering of pencil sketches strewn across her bed. She and John Carruthers were great friends, Hendry said. "She didn't want to stop, but she drifted off again."

Monday night and lights were burning in the bureaus. "Everybody works tonight," MacKenzie said. McKitrick and Gallina were in Santa Rosa.

MacKenzie said, "Our subject didn't have his class picture taken. There's an empty square in his school yearbook. Always the odd man out.

"But the red car has a record. We do better with cars than we do with people. They went back to the paper files in Sacramento, before the computer. The recorded purchaser has a backyard paint shop. He buys and sells old cars. First he paints them. He was a high school classmate of our subject's. The school yearbook describes them as best friends."

Carrie blanched. "So they paint cars together. And get blobs of paint on their shoes."

"Gallina points out we still have to pussyfoot up there. We can't tie that red car to the rapes or the fires." He waved his hand at the map pinned on the wall. "This, Gallina says, is a work of creative fiction."

"What about McKitrick?" Carrie asked.

"Oh, he's like us. He likes intuition. He plods along. They're good men. They make their cases. And they're up there. The red car is all they've got."

She found Kang at the telephone. Washoe and his blond partner had come in. "Come on," Carrie told Kang. "I'll let you drive."

"My father would be proud," Kang said.

It was quiet. In the second hour of their watch, MacKenzie found them and pulled alongside to talk.

"The red car is gone," he said. "It left some time tonight, but McKitrick found her employer in Santa Rosa. She just happens to be Irish."

"Is McKitrick Irish?" Kang asked him.

"He can be," MacKenzie said. "He's old school. When there isn't any warrant, charm will have to do. Our car owner is in Oakland, visiting a sister. The Oakland police have found it. They'll tell us if it moves."

Carrie watched his eyes. "There's more, isn't there?"

MacKenzie nodded. "Her job. The antique shop is

closed for two days twice every month, when she comes down to see her sister. It's always on a Monday and a Tuesday."

"And maybe there's a young man living there," Carrie said.

"Or nearby," MacKenzie said. "We should be able to find out."

"Who works in a car paint shop somewhere," Carrie said.

"Something like that," MacKenzie agreed.

"Maybe in San Francisco," Carrie went on. "Where half the auto paint shops in the city are all around us in the Southern. I don't like it."

"McKitrick and Gallina are driving back," MacKenzie said. "They're going to have somebody make a list of paint shops, match them with commercial laundries that do uniforms. Tomorrow they'll knock on the door in Oakland."

She told Kang, "Let's go watch our streets."

"Before somebody steals them," Kang said.

They patrolled. New bright lights were burning at the bus stops near the senior housing high-rise. To show that the mayor cared. Tuesday dawned, with children off to school.

She slept fitfully, awoke in damp sheets. A little man with pins in his mouth had been dancing all around her with a measuring tape, giant numbers tattooed on his thin arms. She laid out clothes to pack for her four days in the country. MacKenzie was driving them up. Spenser said he'd caught a black bass. He'd invited MacKenzie to dinner. There was a letter from her sister. He'd leave it on the silver tray if he went out.

At the hospital, Elizabeth was sleeping. The drawing

was off to the printer, Hendry said. She seemed relieved. The sweater was finished. It swung on a hanger in the window.

Lights were still bright at midnight in the bureaus above Southern Station. The lot was empty of cars. Even the Hertz cars were out tonight.

MacKenzie said, "The car went out today, two women in it. They went shopping, came back with bags and packages."

"Two gray-haired old ladies, looking helpless and innocent," Kang said. "They'd make good bank robbers."

MacKenzie said, "Except that one has red hair. They said they don't know where her son is. He hasn't told them his address."

She and Kang took turns watching and driving. The Indians were gone. "There must be work somewhere," Kang said. "I'm glad my father has a steady job."

MacKenzie was waiting at the door when they pulled into the lot. The radios had been almost silent for four hours. "It's almost over. When we get back from our weekend they'll have found him. Then we'll know."

In his comfortable old blues, the gold bar at his collar. "They won't even miss us."

She rode beside him in silent comfort, in loose skirt and soft shoes, cool on the smooth leather of the seat. It no longer seemed strange watching the hood of a Mercedes preceding them around the curves of a country road. Her life was filled with new things and new impressions of old things. Riding through the countryside to Spenser's house as a passenger was different and pleasant. Groceries tucked in back. Miles of freeway behind them.

Hawks were circling in the rising heat, watching the long pale golden grass from high above. It wouldn't be as hot today.

The La Pointes passed them, going the other way, on their way to market, Rosalee and Anton. "John will be in school," she said. "He'll hate that. I guess the summer's over."

MacKenzie said, "I remember being ten. That's when the whole world opened up to me. It suddenly got bigger. There were so many things to do."

"Did you think you'd be a policeman?"

157

"Yes. I had a favorite uncle who was. Or I'd be an engineer like my father. Or a lawyer. They're important people in the mountains. Down here they're just quarrelsome. If the war hadn't come along I'd have gone on to school. I wasn't at a loss for choices, and I like the one I made."

She thought, I made it, too, and wondered if their reasons were the same. Some were. He liked a kind of discipline, not the grim-jawed kind. Maybe it was more a sense of order. He wasn't as quick and cutting as Spenser. But he could look stern. Well, enough of that. He was just Ian MacKenzie and he took things seriously. Sometimes he had a twinkle in his eye.

He turned into the lane, then drifted to a stop in the gravel. Rows of pink ladies stood before them, all around the house, pale pink sentinels. Fall was coming.

"That's the color to wear walking in the mountains," he said.

She laughed. "I can't see you in pink."

"Oh no, not me. Someone else."

"I don't wear pink," she said firmly. "Maybe just a cap, in case I got lost. What will you do this weekend?"

"Shop for the house. Get sent on errands by my daughter. Set up books for a young husband who's trying to become a general contractor. I'm glad I like him. It sometimes doesn't work that way."

She said, "I was thinking of asking Spenser to go walking on the beach. It's that time of year. We ought to go out and talk of portentous things.

"But we'll go swimming, too, at the club, if you think you'd like to come, and we have a favorite restaurant for dinner."

"I'll see both of you tonight. You and your uncle. We'll make plans."

Spenser came out to greet them. "You look very nice today," he said. She looked up and felt herself flushing. Spenser didn't often say things like that to her.

"I thought so, too," MacKenzie said.

Suddenly, that's the way she felt. It was most pleasant, she decided, having two men to flatter you. The feeling lasted the whole afternoon.

They talked a long time at dinner, chairs pushed back, before she walked MacKenzie out to his car to go home.

Afterward Spenser said, "Well, what are you going to do about him?"

It startled her. Was he going to start that, too? "Spenser, I don't know what you're talking about. I don't have to do anything about him!"

But he said, "I think I know when a serious man is paying court. I did it once myself."

And he walked out of the room to leave her standing there in anger and in wonder.

She cleared away and got food ready for their walk tomorrow, then walked out into the lane. Cool enough for a sweater. Before long her ears would pick out the night sounds. Spenser, of course, was taking a lot for granted. MacKenzie had never suggested he was serious. He was just there, like Roger. Well, she thought, she liked him there. He had something of her father, an attentiveness, a gravity. Something of Spenser in his crustiness. Something of a stranger. A great deal of that.

No, she supposed she knew MacKenzie as well as she could be expected to, and of course she liked him a great deal. What she didn't know enough about at this moment was what she wanted, if she wanted anything she didn't have.

For now she had this cooling night, the dark like a cloak about her, and the crickets starting, and a touch of moisture in the air after the long dryness. She could be alone and feel comfort in it. She'd walked this lane before. In her war with herself to leave the classrooms and the children and seek new ways to use herself. That much was settled now, and she felt more alive than she ever had before.

She and Spenser walked in the hard sand, the morning fog around them and the waves at their feet.

She said, "I guess I only want to know about myself."

"We all should," Spenser said.

"You always said I was the ultimate source and you were just a well-informed observer. But you do help me sort things out."

Spenser said, "I think I've already been told you have no interest in making a choice about a man in your life."

"That's right. There's none to make," she said sharply.

"Very well. Just life. Your uncaught criminal, among other things."

She said grimly, "I don't want him on my streets. That's all." Then laughed. "I sound as tough as Bullard. But that's part of it. Who I am. Alkron's using all her wiles to get into the bureaus. She looks forward to being an inspector. So does Roger, but he's not impatient. MacKenzie tells him to stay on the street awhile and learn the business. Sometimes the bureaus just reach down and pluck you away, like Leong with her phenomenal memory.

"MacKenzie thinks I can get into Juvenile at any time. I could work with the schools. I speak their language and I'd be useful there. I could teach at the Academy, too. Our conversations don't get much beyond that when we talk about it, MacKenzie and I."

"He won't tell you what to do?"

"I guess it's that. I could always go to vice crimes and lure johns on street corners. Roger laughs at that. He said I'd just step up and confess I was a cop. I have no guile."

"Thank God for that," Spenser said.

"I thought it was enough just to be a cop. That was hard enough to decide. Now they're throwing choices at me and I'm supposed to tell them something.

"What everybody overlooks is that I like what I'm doing, and I like the cops who do it. In school I got to know the children better at the recess. I used to volunteer when other teachers wanted to just sit and have a smoke. I think I like to be where all the action is.

"You know, I remember sitting in the teachers' room trying to make conversation, and even with the windows closed I could hear them out there. My mind kept drifting out the windows.

"When I was growing up I did that. I'd be studying and the voices would come in the window and I'd say, 'Uh-oh, they're going to get in trouble over that,' and I'd be out the door. I'd have to sit up half the night getting homework done while all the rest of the house was asleep, safely tucked away. Like everybody's parent.

"The point is, soon I'll take the sergeants' exam, and I'll do well on that. I'm physically capable and I've had good teachers on the street. I'll make sergeant in my fourth year. It isn't like MacKenzie's day. It took eight years then.

"And he'll be there. He'll be my lieutenant or my captain."

They rounded the point cautiously, the tide rising, washing over the narrow strip of sand.

"Let's have lunch," Spenser said.

They stretched their legs for the last half mile along the sand, then climbed carefully up the unstable shale face of the fifty feet of ocean cliff and scrambled up together to sit at the cliff's edge.

The sky was blue now. The mist had burned away and the whole ocean lay before them, pale green and cut with froth, and the sharp smells of salt and decaying kelp rose up to them.

"MacKenzie said we just keep the parades marching and the traffic sorted out. We shouldn't complicate it. I guess I want to keep MacKenzie's parades moving, and do what Bullard does, and stand there like Roger does, patiently. MacKenzie will be there somewhere."

"Well," Spenser said, "I watched you leave the schoolchildren you were fond of. You had reasons, some of which I knew. I think I also visualized you on a quest for a companion and a warrior you'd find somewhere along the way, someone doing the same things you are. At least, I'd hoped you'd come to that. You could have settled long ago for one of your young men of small vision."

"Is that selfish?"

"Purposeful, I like to think."

But her mind was still on his last words. She hadn't answered him. Companion and warrior. Was that what she was looking for?

She said, "This is where we sat the day I told you I was going to be a policeman."

"Where your decisions are announced. You've usually got your mind made up before we get here, I believe."

"Not always. Sometimes it's as if I need to come up here to learn what I've known all along. I need to see the whole world stretching away to see what's right in front of me."

"Maybe," Spenser said. "Maybe you have to see clearly the good sense in it. And the glory."

They were deep in their own thoughts. When he next looked at her, she was smiling.

"What?" he said. "Something funny?"

"No. Just a small thought. I'll tell you, maybe, someday. It's about some rabbits."

It was time to cook up the last of the summer tomatoes from Rosalee's yellowing vines with basil from the garden to freeze against the winter. To cut back the summer flowers and clear the garden for winter.

She walked in the grape arbor behind the barn, busy with bees suddenly, and angry yellow jackets, to finger the fat Concord grapes. Next time she came she'd make jelly for the cooler and the church fair.

They went to church on Sunday, a time of walking slowly up the long path through the lawns and greeting old friends, everyone in crisp summer clothes.

Groups formed around Spenser for brief words as they walked through. Here Spenser was the local member of the water board and a man who made hard sense of figures and unfriendly and obscure fiscal laws.

"Giver of water and guardian of the nuts stored for winter," Spenser said. This valley was his boardroom now.

These were neighbors and the parents whose children she had taught at the little school. The familiar faces. She did not see them as often now. Everyone had a nice scrubbed look.

But they'd changed, too, since she'd arrived here from the university eager for the first classroom of her own and pleased to find one in her own community. Spenser's white thatch stood out, but many heads were graying now. That surprised her. She'd never thought of it. Spenser was growing older. And so, she supposed, was she.

Many had seen her picture in the paper. That already seemed a long time ago. "We don't see you often enough in church in your new job, Ms. Lubick." Dr. Wesley Phelps met them at the door. "The schedule," she said. "I'm not home that much anymore."

He was not much older than she, blond hair too long for his collar, already thinning. She wasn't sure he approved of policemen. Part of his generation. He'd been taken into a church that had been built fifty years ago and kept strong by its congregation. No new church to be built, no grand battles to be fought. The desperate poor he spoke of were far away. He formed groups of parents to deal with today's scourges—children using drugs; divorce and remarriage; and mixed-up families spread out over the valley community. He had his problems, too.

He beamed at her. "We're sending our contribution to your St. Anthony Dining Room," he told her. "For all those holiday meals over Christmas. And this year we're shipping off crates of fresh apples."

Oh, God, she thought. The windows. Apple fights in the Southern.

"They'll make a lot of apple pies." The clergyman spoke with rapt sincerity.

She shook his hand.

"I understand they'll need some volunteers to cook them," Dr. Phelps said. "I can recommend you, you know, as a resident pie maker."

She pictured herself in police blues, covered with white flour, surprised faces staring through a window. She looked at the minister again. Maybe she'd underestimated him.

The pink ladies stood sentinel around the house on naked stalks. A time of year. The next time she came they'd be drooping, nearly gone, and Spenser would clip the stalks away for compost. Then the calla lilies would push up to blossom whitely through the winter rains.

Spenser said, "I'll fix the supper. MacKenzie be here about nine?"

"Yes. He said nine."

The day drifted by. She couldn't keep her mind on her book today. She woke from time to time to hear Spenser on the phone.

She was asleep·when he opened her door to say dinner was ready and MacKenzie on the way.

He drove through the soft night. It was pleasant riding with him through black tunnels in the tall redwoods that marked the end of apple country before the road lifted into the round hills, pale in moonlight. Beyond, they dipped down again toward the glow in the sky of freeway lights and the distant city.

MacKenzie talked about the young officer in Santa Rosa who'd been knocking on so many doors. "He paints a picture of a rapist. He knows that. But he also knows it might not be true. He and the captain. They've all got to be careful.

"Still, it fits. His childhood, his mother's treatment of him. His aloofness.

"The captain's another storyteller. You like those. He said it reminds him of a dog poisoner there, a banker and churchgoer, known and respected. But he kept moving to different parts of town. Each new house was like the last. Around each house, after a time, the dog poisoning began again. Through the neighborhood.

"The captain had no evidence, but he knew. He won-

167

dered if the man's family didn't know, too. Even if they just knew they were different.

"The man's children were growing. He became an officer in his bank, president of the Rotary. But his wife seemed to have no friends. His children would go home from school and the door would close behind them. No other children went to play.

"In the fourth house they lived in he was caught dropping hamburger laced with rat poison over the back fence, onto the path in the grass the neighbor's dogs wore charging back and forth. The neighbor was an old friend of the captain's. He'd been watching out his window."

Carrie said, "He thinks this is the same?"

"Their isolation is the same. Police have chatted up the neighbors all around her former homes. Nobody ever came to call. My friend has not learned much about them. That's something to know. They are reclusive. But it leaves us with just two possibilities, the mother and the school friend who paints cars.

"The captain thinks the mother will never talk to us. He's left with the friend. They're working on him. They're knocking on doors, tracing a whole high school class, looking for someone with an old snapshot.

"In Oakland, police are talking to the aunt. The boy lived there for several months while he worked at a car paint shop in Oakland. One day she found a note that he was moving, he'd found a better job."

"Won't she tell us?"

"She doesn't know. She and her sister never talk about him. They never have. She feels guilty about that, but she's glad he's gone. He always made her feel uncomfortable, even when he was a child."

"What do we do about all that?"

"Work on the friend. One day they'll knock on the door and he'll begin to talk. We just don't know what day that will be."

Carrie said, "Those sisters. They're together every two weeks. They go out shopping, and they go home. They sit and talk, but never about the only man in their family, a son and nephew. As if he didn't exist. How very sad. Was the banker's wife like that too?"

"Maybe just like that."

"And we just wait."

"We watch our backyard fences," MacKenzie said.

They rode in silence until Carrie said, "You've believed in the red car all along, haven't you?"

She studied his face. MacKenzie and his three girl cops.

Now he smiled. "Something told me you were right."

She turned away and saw they were drumming up the last long grade, now topping it, the city laid out before them in its necklaces of streetlights going up and over the tall hills, standing in white mist above the blackness of the bay, a city perched on a mystic cloud.

At her door, he said, "I'll go straight in. I'll change down there."

She walked inside and began changing into her blues and strapping on her gear.

Roger was driving slowly past the church when a movement at the corner of her eye made Carrie turn. She heard thin, high screams begin. She switched on the flood and the flasher. Their doors slammed simultaneously. A girl with long black hair was stumbling toward them through the rubble of the parking lot, in the whiteness of the floodlight, screaming as she ran. A young man ran behind her, a hobbled, gimpy run, his pants and parka white with brick dust. The girl threw herself into Roger's arms.

She talked and sobbed. "Three men in a pickup truck. It was green. They beat him up and took our things away!"

"What kind of pickup? New or old?" Carrie asked the boy.

His face seemed stiff. "GMC. Five years old about. The plates were white. I think Oregon."

It was hurting him to talk. The girl was still sobbing in Roger's arms.

Carrie took the boy's chin in her hand and examined his face. It was scuffed and already starting to swell along his jawline. Like the girl, he wore an expensive padded parka and jeans. God, Carrie thought, he looks like he's been kicked.

He wasn't as tall as she was.

"They did this with their feet?" she asked.

"They're lumberjacks. They were wearing big boots." She heard Roger putting it out on the air, calling for an ambulance. The girl was still clutching at him. "They took my expensive sleeping bag, an Arctic. It was blue. Light blue. My pack was light blue, too, and it's got all my clothes. They're matching. My mother got them for me to go camping."

Carrie sat the boy down on the curb and asked his name, wrote the letters as he mumbled them. His jaw was hurt. His whole face was a mess. His mouth was bleeding. But he said, "They all had her. I heard them. They took turns. They're bigger than I am!" He was crying.

The girl was chattering at Roger, touching him. "They gave us a ride from Healdsburg. That's where we live. We told them we were coming down for this religious experience in the commune but they didn't take us like they promised. They just brought us here."

Carrie asked, "Did they all rape you?"

The boy said, "They took her in the truck and they kept kicking me."

He was beginning to shudder. Carrie put an arm around his shoulders. When the ambulance pulled up, she called out, "This one first. We'll need a blanket." She helped him to his feet.

The girl was standing, straightening her clothes. She had waist-length hair and a pretty face. There was no brick dust on her clothes.

The medic had a blanket over the boy's shoulders and was helping him up the step into the ambulance.

"How did you meet these men?" Carrie asked.

"We were hitchhiking down to this commune in Marin County, one I heard of, and they said they'd take us there. We were at that all-night gas station where we live, in Healdsburg. The boy there knows me. He can tell you. They bought us hamburgers at McDonald's but they kept on driving. They said they didn't have enough gas to drive around in the mountains looking for the commune and we'd have to go back on our own in the morning. But they had lots of money. They had big bills in their wallets."

"Did they rob you?"

She was startled. "No."

"But they raped you."

"They made me get out of the back of the truck and in the cab. They made me pull down my pants and they did it on the seat. When we parked over there." She pointed out beyond the parking lot.

God, she was tiny, Carrie thought.

"Can you describe them?"

"They were all big, I know that. The one who owned the truck was the biggest. It was his truck. They were all taller than that officer." She meant Roger. She described their Pendletons, jeans, big belt buckles, cowboy boots with pointed toes, cowboy hats.

Carrie asked, "Do your parents know where you are?"

"I've only got a mother. She knows all about the commune. She said it would be good for me. I'm old enough."

"How old?"

"I'm eighteen."

"Do you live with your mother in Healdsburg?"

"Yes, and she knows I planned to come down here. I've been planning it a long time. We just didn't decide when. But today Bobby said he'd come with me and we just packed and came. I left a note. Do you have to tell my mother?"

"I don't know. Not if you're eighteen. If you don't want us to. We'll talk about it. I should think you'd want her to know."

"She'd feel awful if she knew I lost that sleeping bag. It cost an awful lot."

"You'll both go to the hospital first," Carrie said. "You'll be checked over."

"I need a place to tidy up," the girl said.

The medic had been watching, listening. "If you'll ride along," he said. "We'd better get him in."

"Give me a minute," Carrie said.

She'd been hearing the murmur of voices from the Southern cars. Going to the freeway entrances. "They'll be long gone from here," a voice said. "Tell the highway patrol."

"We'll take the truck stop," she heard Alkron say.

She rode in the ambulance. At the Central, the girl marched through the swinging doors and the steward helped the boy inside.

Carrie turned the girl over to the nurse in the white jumpsuit. "Multiple rape," she said. "I'm not clear how many."

Roger was outside. "Your friend Alkron got them," he said. "I heard her crowing."

They drove to the truck stop and saw three young men

standing in the flood from Alkron's car, faces to the station wall, hands handcuffed behind them. Boots and felt cowboy hats. The dark green GMC was parked in the semidarkness behind the station.

"I caught them with their pants down. They were busy washing their private parts in the public sink. They said they were always careful to do that."

MacKenzie was there, watching. The other cars were pulling out.

"They're all insisting they paid for it," Alkron told MacKenzie. "They said they knew they'd have to do that down here. They brought plenty of money for sex and beer and gas for the truck. They said the boyfriend started whining about it so they rolled him around a little in the dirt."

MacKenzie said, "Get the wagon. Let's get them in. How old is she?" he asked Carrie.

"She said eighteen. She doesn't look it."

Roger was right. Alkron was crowing. "I knew they'd be here. These boys came to see the city lights. We've got more lights here than any other place in the Southern!"

The pickup bed was a jumble of sleeping bags and packs and trash. Alkron started pulling things apart, notebook in hand, making a list. "Six Hawaiian Punch cans. One spare tire and wheel not bolted down. Five sleeping bags, one of them a pretty blue. Sixteen candy wrappers."

Carrie told MacKenzie, "He has toe marks on his clothes. I think he was kicked in the face. His jaw could be broken." She added, "The girl is nice and clean."

"All right," MacKenzie said. "When she can travel, bring her in. Let me know about the boy. If they release him, keep them separated."

The nurse was waiting for them. She handed Carrie two large, sealed envelopes. "Personal effects. Your medical stuff all tagged for evidence. The report's inside. The doctor said he's got enough semen for lots more rape cases if you're ever short. Healthy young men."

Carrie noted the names of the nurse and doctor attending, then the numbers, times in and out.

"She's yours any time you want her. She's in there now telling the trauma team all about her commune. She doesn't know beans, does she?"

"I don't know yet," Carrie said. Writing bare essentials in her notebook. From the envelope. Hair color, eyes, height, weight, date of birth. One hundred two pounds.

"We'll have a trip to Juvenile," she told Roger. "She's sixteen."

"She didn't want the counseling," the nurse said. "She doesn't have any bad feelings about it."

Then the girl walked out the door, neatly buttoned, long hair brushed. A child. A very pretty child. With something missing.

"We've got your sleeping bag and clothes," Roger told her. She smiled. Suddenly strikingly beautiful. Even the tough nurse noticed. She said gently, "We're going to have to keep your friend. His jaw has to be wired. He'll be drinking through a straw."

She didn't seem to hear. She was talking to Roger. ". . . all my clothes. I thought I'd have them all hanging up by now. Those boys said they'd take us. If they hadn't promised I surely wouldn't have climbed into the back of that old truck."

She said, "I know my mother's going to be relieved."

Carrie began to get that feeling.

"Did you lie to me about your age?" she asked the girl.

"My mother considers me grown up. I have a job, and I help her cook and clean. We take care of one another." Standing next to Roger.

Carrie took her by the arm and started moving her outside. An act of rescue.

MacKenzie was back when they got there. McDowell was on the street. The new sergeant, Harris, was inside, and the station keeper. The three boys, in stocking feet, were handcuffed to the wooden bench. Not arrogant now. Their boots were in a corner, tagged for evidence.

"Take her in my office," MacKenzie said. "Talk to her in there."

Carrie said, "Tell Alkron she's got a statutory rape. In addition to whatever else."

MacKenzie sighed. "You'd better call her mother. I'll call Juvenile Hall and tell them we're coming."

"We've also got a broken jaw," Carrie said. She pointed to the boots.

She put the girl in the wooden chair and sat at the desk to fill in the forms. "Let's do this again from the beginning. Full name, date of birth, mother's name, address. All that. I'll check what you tell me against your operator's license and any other ID you're carrying."

She found the operator's license, four months old. She was sixteen. Also in her wallet a stack of old currency in small bills, thirty-two dollars. And three crisp new ten-dollar bills.

"Those new ones aren't mine, you know," the girl said. "They're contributions to the commune. They like to have you bring some money to help out. That's what I heard."

Carrie said, "Were you going to give the boys a receipt? To take it off their income tax?"

"If it's appropriate. I don't know about that. I'm sure the commune would if they mentioned it."

Her mother sounded all right on the phone. Sleepy. Awakened by the telephone. She didn't seem surprised. "I don't know what to do with her. I've had her on the pill since she was twelve. Sometimes I think she doesn't even know she's doing it. She's always been a normal child except for that. Maybe too pretty and not very bright, but she's very sweet. I supposed the commune would be one way. Before she gets everyone up here put in jail."

"All right," Carrie said. "I'll put her down as an out-of-control juvenile and they'll hold her until you come down and make arrangements. They'll want to talk to you about it."

She told the mother about the boy.

"I knew who she was going off with. He's a nice boy. I know his parents. I'd better telephone so they'll know where he is."

Carrie gave her the addresses and phone numbers.

At the last the mother said, "She left a note where she was going. She's always been thoughtful about that."

Then Carrie put the girl on. She assured her mother the sleeping bag was safe. She told her mother, "Those lumberjacks would have taken all our things if the police hadn't stopped them!" Indignantly. She didn't say a word about the rape.

Outside, Carrie told Alkron, "You've got a statutory and a felony assault with boots. The girl is sixteen. The

177

boy will be at County General. You write the arrest as a supplemental. I'll give you all the numbers."

Alkron unlocked the boys from the prisoners' bench but handcuffed them together. "On your feet!" she ordered.

"I told you we paid that girl," one of the boys complained.

Alkron looked at them disgustedly. "You should have checked her age. That makes it a crime, even if you threw in the truck."

MacKenzie said, singling out the driver, "I talked to your brother. He's filing a complaint in Oregon. He said you didn't have permission to drive the truck."

"Shit," the boy drawled. "He always lets me drive it. He's got a brand-new one."

"This way," Alkron said, "the insurance buys the gas when he drives it home. Smart brother."

"Where were you going?" MacKenzie asked them.

"We're coming down to get jobs in the oil fields. They don't pay too good in Salem. I work in a gas station. We've been saving up." He looked hopefully at MacKenzie.

"I advised your brother to call your families. They'll have to get a lawyer. Your brother will come down and get the pickup." MacKenzie spoke plainly, almost with regret.

Alkron herded them out the door. Without their boots, they were no taller than she was. Toward the elevator and city prison, five floors overhead.

"You guys," she said. "There hasn't been a new oil field in Southern California in forty years."

Carrie went back to her reports. She asked the girl to

start again, at the beginning. She did. She told it all, lucidly, obligingly.

"They'll take good care of you over there," Carrie told her. "Until your mother comes."

"Of course they will," she assured Carrie.

Driving back from Juvenile Hall, Roger took note of the temperature on the Delta Airlines billboard. Not alarming yet, he said. The nighttime coolness just hadn't settled in.

The tension of the early hours had gone. The special shifts that marked the waiting and the watching had gone home. They heard laughter on the channel and a bored, dry, disapproving voice laconically sending a car here, another there, ignoring levity.

MacKenzie was in his office reading their reports.

"It finally caught up with me," Carrie said. "The mother knows but she wouldn't say. She's got a seven-year-old daughter in a sixteen-year-old body. She's so beautiful."

MacKenzie said, "The court won't let her just go home. The process will start here. There's a medical record up there somewhere. The doctors will put it all together."

Carrie smiled at him. "Do you ever think, There but for the grace of God?"

"Mine lost their drivers' licenses for speeding. In other ways, they're remarkably honorable young men."

He signed the reports. "They'll take care of her."

At the door, Wellington backed into them, dragging an eight-foot marijuana plant into the room. Gillespie walked behind, holding by the elbow an eighty-year-old man who smiled pleasantly around the room.

Gillespie said, "I don't believe it yet. But here's part of it."

"He just walked up to the car and asked us up to see his garden," Wellington said. "So we went. He's got a greenhouse up there on the roof of his crummy building. You got to walk up four flights and climb a ladder, and he's got roses, tomatoes, artichokes, and a field of marijuana. They're not plants, they're trees. He thinks they're pretty. Says all the young people come up to admire them. He gives them souvenirs."

"He's got twelve trees up there," Gillespie said. "We brought one with us so you wouldn't think we were chewing this stuff with our lunch."

The watches were coming in for their relief. Someone dug a red jacket out of the school lost-and-found box and hung it on a branch. Someone else found a green stocking. The dignified Ed Wellington stood there grinning like an idiot.

The chatter slowed and stopped and Carrie looked up

to see MacKenzie there, looking like a benign school principal.

"Use the dolly when you take that upstairs. Get one from the basement. Otherwise, you'll leave a trail of evidence. Once Narcotics removes the plants, cite this gentleman and take him home. Don't let them leave him in a mess if you can help it. Explain that he's got to come to court. Explain you'll pick him up and bring him. Clear?"

Wellington, sober now, said, "They might make a fuss up there. You know how they are."

"Tell them that's the way I want it," MacKenzie said. Then he walked out the door.

Carrie and Roger followed.

In their car, watching their streets, she said, "He makes it all so simple. I think it's all muddled up and hopeless and he says something like, 'Put that in your report,' and somehow I feel better, but I'm darned if I know why."

Roger said, "It is simple. Traffic is moving. The parade is going by. The little kids are waving. It's all in hand. That's why we're here."

The doughnut shop was filling up with people waiting for the first batch of hot doughnuts. Even in the summer. On the corner the unpainted shelves of the sidewalk boot shop were empty but for windblown trash. Men and women were stirring in their doorways, though it was not yet dawn. Soon people would start leaving for their early morning jobs. The dawn burglar alarms would light up lights at the security firms. The children would start off for school.

No, she told Spenser later in the day. Nothing new. They were still looking, up there in the bureaus. The night streets were full of cops. Some hadn't worked the streets in years.

He was off to Sacramento the next day on water business. His farmers needed a better handle on the water sources. They didn't want a federal project, no massive dams to set new laws and bureaucrats to work designing new forms to fill out. He was going to tell them once again, they were just small farmers, wanting enough water. Not wanting to continue losing their share to the growing subdivisions.

She told him MacKenzie had decided it was time for him to leave his Santa Rosa family alone, let them run things for themselves.

"We could invite him up," she said. "He likes the swimming."

"Why not?" Spenser agreed.

"There's the spare room. It's just that walking in the lane with us might be a little tame. He likes mountains.

"Why didn't we do that?" she said. "We went skiing at Squaw Valley but we never tried the open trails."

"There weren't any pretty girls," Spenser said.

"MacKenzie goes skiing on Mount Lassen. Did I tell you that? He sleeps out on the mountain, in the snow. He used to take his children."

"He's a man of the mountains," Spenser said.

"Well, we'll see you in a few days," she said. "Maybe it will all be over. I'll invite him up. We can drive up together. It saves gas."

"Most sensible," her uncle said.

The day was already growing warm when she slipped between the sheets. She would call Alkron later and tell her about the little tailor. She might call Roger and see if he'd like dinner at the Vietnamese place.

T he heat of the afternoon had intensified by nightfall. She took a short run, then showered and dressed in cool clothes. MacKenzie called to say he was already there. Things were happening. She said, "There's a hot wind blowing. And it's Monday."

He said, "I've spent the day up in the bureaus. Our unbalanced friend might never get another night."

The child's drawing stared at her when she walked in the door. Nobody had even pinned a used-car sales pitch over it. She would know him anywhere.

The rooms inside were still cool but the heat would penetrate here, too, by midnight. Sergeant McDowell handled the lineup. MacKenzie was upstairs.

"Watch for piles of combustibles blown into corners," he intoned. "Public Works will circulate through the neighborhoods. If you see a pile of trash, call it in. We'll send a truck. All the bureau cars will be on the street. Watch for the red car, and make no solo stops. Call for backup."

The swing watch was still working a missing person in the motel on Seventh Street. A diamond salesman, missing with his briefcase and his samples, leaving behind clothes and notebooks and an empty wallet. His driver's license missing, his credit cards, and his rental car.

Washoe growled, "The car'll be in Reno. He'll be in a ditch."

"The lieutenant said to inform you the little girl, Elizabeth, has gone home from the hospital and is with her parents. Any heavy breathers in the shrubbery around her parents' house will be police officers. The night supervising captain has advised, don't go by. He might be standing there to hand out five-day vacations without pay. Clear?"

They drifted out in silence. It was thirty minutes before midnight.

Carrie and Roger started with their alleys, cutting through in zigzags. Headquarters was murmuring low-priority calls left from the swing watch. None for them. Their streets were quiet.

Roger flipped his hat into the back seat. The hot wind was blowing backward, from the inland valleys, not the sea. Blowing in vast sweeping circles all around the fringes of the bay, blowing through the cities that bounded it for almost a hundred miles, blowing through its salt marshes as far down as San Jose and over barren hills as far north as Petaluma, mixing the smells of factory smokestacks with odors of pesticides and cow barns and the rot of slums and dirty streets, settling here to blow street grit and pieces of paper around in little eddies where two winds met at street corners.

The call from headquarters came out of the silence. It startled both of them.

"Boy Four. We have a complaint unknown. The caller is a woman, perhaps a Vietnamese. She called for the officer with the candy. She said you have met her daughters. Is that you, Boy Four? Boy Five, Officer Alkron?"

Carrie held the mike. "The call is for Boy Four, Headquarters. The address is a warehouse at Sixth and Elsie. I will inform you of the street address. This is our call, Headquarters."

"It's the alley," she told Roger. "With the cat."

He had already turned and headed for it. She jammed the clipboard into its slot on the dash so it wouldn't rattle, touched the stick near her hand. Headquarters was still talking.

"The complainant said there is no injury to her children. No ambulance is required. She will tell the tall woman officer who carries candies, Boy Four."

"Let's park in the alley."

Roger pulled into the alley mouth, flicked the flood on and off. There was no one in the alley. Cars were parked half on the sidewalks on both sides. They got out together, doors clicking shut behind them. She had the long flashlight. The dark houses rose over them as they walked. Not even a television going.

Carrie said, "The doors are on the inside courtyard. There are no lights in there."

"If there were, they'd be burned out," Roger said.

Dim lights from apartment windows overhead. She swept her light once around the courtyard. Sixty by sixty. No one was there. Three upper rows of windows. Some were lighted. Porches down below, and stairwells. Everything was bare and dark. Clothes hanging against the sky. She turned to the left and three lighted windows, closed now, the blinds drawn. Up two steps to the wooden porch. Roger was at her right shoulder, six feet behind. She flicked off the light and tapped lightly at the door.

"It's Officer Carrie. There is another policeman with me. It's all right to open."

A shade moved at the window as someone looked outside. The door was opened by a slim woman with grave eyes, long hair like her daughters, in shirt and jeans and soft shoes.

She said, "I'm glad you are the one who came. My children know you. They said you watch them go to school, and you look after them. I'm very grateful." She held the door wide for Carrie. "It's all right. We are alone."

Roger said, "I'll be outside."

The girls were in their nightclothes. They looked frightened. Carrie dropped to her knees and reached out for them. Her arms circled them. "You're all right?"

The taller one said, "Yes, but Jacqueline got pinched. On her arm. Look, it made an awful mark."

The smaller child held up her arm, a blue bruise, the work of two big, vicious fingers, blue and swelling.

"I have put some ice," the mother said.

"Who?" Carrie asked. "Someone you know?"

"No. He goes by here every day but we do not know him. Tonight he came in the window and the children screamed. I ran in with the broom and he ran away. But we know him. He walks in the alley. His picture is right here, in the paper."

The drawing stared at Carrie from the table, beneath a table lamp, the man small and stark on newsprint, with those eyes.

"He was very angry because our mother hit him with the broom, and he pinched Jacqueline and ran away!"

She got to her feet, opened the door a crack.

"Roger, our madman was here! He climbed in a window and they chased him out again! They're all right, but he was here! They've identified him from the picture in the paper. I'll get details. You'd better put it out."

Roger looked at her. He said, "He's going to be one frustrated crazy, now."

Carrie shut the door and gathered the girls to her. Her girls! He was on their street! She pulled out her notebook.

"Tell me!" She wrote their names. Jacqueline, Suzanne, their mother, Suzette Mai. The children's hands reached out to touch her sleeves, the backs of her hands. She printed carefully.

"We knew we must call," the mother said. "We saw it in the paper, and it was already old. But it was late. We were going to call tomorrow because we were not sure. We thought it might be the same man who walks by. We were not certain.

"When they were screaming and I turned on the light, I saw him. As close as you are to me. It is the man!"

Suzanne said proudly, "Our mother chased him! He ran down the street and she chased him with the broom!"

"You chased him?" This beautiful woman was scarcely bigger than her children.

"I followed him. I was angry! He ran to the corner! He went to that hotel with the gold printing on the door! He had a key to go inside! I saw him go up the stairs!

"Then I came back and called for you!"

Carrie looked at the three of them, amazed. "You chased him with a broom."

The woman shrugged slim shoulders. "I have no husband now."

"We'll find him," Carrie said. "I'll come and tap on the door. It will be very late. Look out the window to make sure."

She opened the door to find Roger there. He said, "There's a fire. I can't raise them on the pic. The channel's in a mess. I'll have to use the car."

"We know where he is!" Carrie told him. "She followed him to the Excelsior Hotel. He had a key, so he's got a room. He climbed the stairs. They'd better know! I'll get there through the alley."

"No heroics," Roger said. "Wait for me." He ran. She heard him back the radio car into the street. She heard fire sirens, too. She walked to the alley, turned toward Sixth Street. She began to jog, then run. She ran faster. Ahead of her, at the end of this dark tunnel, she saw the red flashing lights and the fire engines and long ladder trucks in a jumble. Now she smelled the smoke, a foul stench in her nose and mouth, and the sirens were still coming. The street ahead was a mess. Roger would never make it with the radio car. She ran into a roar of sound that drowned the sound of her running. Smoke was already rolling into the alley mouth. She saw white hoses honeycombed against the wet blackness of the street, fountains of water spraying from the joints.

She ran faster, holding down her flapping gun. She missed the banging of her wood baton at her other leg, remembered fleetingly she'd left it there with Roger on the car seat. So much for training. She broke out of the alley mouth into a chaos of heat and smoke in the broad street. Flames roared at her left, the sound of glass breaking. She didn't look that way. To her right, squads of firemen were trotting down the street with coils of hose, toward the flames. The air was filled with roaring engines and blaring radios crackling with static and urgent voices. She picked footfalls between the fat hoses, dodging firemen, running through thin sheets of spray. At a dead run now. And saw it again, the vicious streak of blue and purple on that slim arm. He had pinched her. The bastard pinched that child!

She ran headlong, pounding through clusters of bystanders at the curb and along the sidewalk, a tall young woman in a dark blue uniform with her hat pulled down over short dark hair, her face intent on a doorway still a quarter of a block away, running to pry out a crazed man who filled her with outrage and with fear.

She knew the door. She had to push through faces hypnotized by scenes of fire behind her and felt rather than saw familiar faces turning to her in surprise. She rattled the locked door and rapped smartly on the glass until, through the scratched gilt, she saw slippered feet coming down the stairs, the sari, and the East Indian woman who reached to unlock the door.

"A young man with long blond hair. He was followed here half an hour ago. He had a key to this door. Where is he?!"

A sibilant, "Yes. He lives here. Room three hundred twelve."

Carrie said, "Call nine-one-one. Tell them an officer needs a backup. Is making an arrest. Can you do that?"

"Yes, I will." The bright knowing eyes.

Carrie brushed past and pounded up the stairs, heard the woman coming up behind her. Familiar faces in the lobby. She pushed through. Procedures and training were forgotten now. She had no thought of caution. He was there and she was going up these stairs to pry him out! She scarcely heard the soft voice of the woman calling after her, "His mother is there, too."

She rattled up the stairs. At the top she looked at the numbers, 304, 306, down to her right. There. That one! Again dimly, she heard other doors opening along the corridor. The fingers of her right hand brushed at the leather of her holstered gun. With the knuckles of her left hand she reached up and rapped sharply at the door.

"Open up in there! Police!"

She raised her hand to rap again when the door swung open and she looked down, a full head below her face, into the eyes of the young man in the drawing. Except for the smile. Long blond hair hanging damply to his shoulders. She thought, He's washed his damned hair! And he's smiling!

Carrie said, "I've come for you! I'm arresting you for assault on a child!"

And stepped into the room, forcing him to step back inside. Her right hand brushed the gun then lifted to reach out for him, hand running down his arm to a thin, childlike wrist, pulling, turning him as her left hand swept back for handcuffs at her belt.

The door slammed shut behind her and a huge bulk thrust her aside as two hands pushed him out of her grasp, propelled him backward across the small room into a corner. He struck the wall and slid down to the floor, surprise and hurt on his face.

The bulk wheeled on Carrie, fat face trembling with rage, as tall or taller than the policewoman, red hair turning white, mottled arms as big as thighs.

Carrie said, "Your son was followed here. I'm arresting him and taking him to jail."

The cheeks were blotched with red, small green eyes sunk in fat. The bulk reached out for Carrie with both arms and slammed the heel of one hand against her face, the other into her shoulder, turning her, then slamming her again with both hands back into the wall. Carrie's eyes were blinded suddenly with tears and the shock of pain in her nose, but saw that huge bulk move in to pin her, those hands still slamming her, until she was held tight against the wall by all that heaving fat until she was engulfed in it, struggling to breathe.

A pounding started at the door. The doorknob rattled. Voices there. The bulk hesitated and Carrie twisted one shoulder back against the solid wall, levering, arms pinned, until she could pull up one knee to slam down hard with one heavy shoe, felt softness under her hard heel, felt the massive weight hesitate, then did it again, and turned against the lever of her shoulder on the wall to sink a fist into the middle of that fat, and again, more room now, braced against the wall, once more! The fat face said, "Oof!" The bulk sagged. Carrie hit her once again, her arm back now all the way and struck with all her strength, then slammed a knee upward against a kneecap, and as the woman started to dip downward, grabbed a fat arm and swung behind, kneeing her again, knee behind a knee, until the bulk gave way, then rode her crashing to the floor. Outside, someone was still pounding on the door. Hand back for handcuffs. Wrenching up one arm, then the other, cuffing them. And sat on that limp bulk, breathing, looking stupidly at that crazy boy crouched in the corner, as the door splintered open and Roger and MacKenzie charged into the room.

MacKenzie gripped her shoulder with one hand, steadied her. Roger went to the corner and pulled the boy to his feet, turned him and clicked on handcuffs.

Her nose felt enormous. It throbbed and she smelled blood, tasted blood. Her own. Her right cheek burned and she touched it. Blood there.

"Your cheek is bleeding," MacKenzie said. "Everything else work all right?"

"I don't know." It hurt to talk. He helped her up and between them they raised the gasping woman to her feet.

Alkron was in the room with Washoe. Alkron reached down and picked up Carrie's hat. It didn't look new anymore. "You broke all the rules," Alkron said. "You're supposed to keep this on your head," she said, and stuck it back on, gently. McKitrick and Gallina were there. The room was full of cops.

Gallina said, "I see you waited for us, as we all agreed. Congratulations. We just came up to serve a warrant. Take someone to jail. We didn't come up here to get mixed up in a riot."

He waved some papers, folded them and took two steps across the room to shove them into the boy's cuffed hand. "You're under arrest, kid. Six felonies. We're going to add some more."

He looked around the room. "There's also a search warrant for this room. You can stand there and watch me do it."

He turned to Mackenzie. "You were invited as a courtesy. Instead your people bull their way in here and make a mess of the whole thing!"

Carrie said loudly, "I arrested him! He is charged with assault on a child and I've got a five-year-old victim and two witnesses. My witness followed him to this hotel."

It hurt to talk but she was mad. She stood eye-to-eye with him. "This is my neighborhood, my crime, and my arrest!"

Gallina looked at her with those inspector's eyes. "Okay," he said at last. "You arrested him. And a big fat mess you made of it."

Alkron began to ease the sobbing bulk of the mother to the door, helped by an ambulance steward. "We'll take her to Central. Let a doctor look at her. I'll book her for resisting, interfering, harboring and felony assault on a police officer."

"That sounds like enough," MacKenzie said. Carrie saw that he was smiling, but he regarded her with concern. She thought, I got myself into a mess and I nearly didn't get myself out of it. She felt battered, and wiped at the blood on her cheek with the back of her hand.

"Old cops," she said with a stiff mouth, "warn us about crazy women."

"I think you met a mother bear," Roger said.

Roger held the prisoner loosely. The boy was slumped over, eyes on the floor.

MacKenzie said, "We're short of cars. I've had everybody at the fire, going through the buildings. I don't even know how all of you got here."

Washoe said, "Headquarters got bombarded. Officer needs assistance. In five languages. The whole street was dropping their own dimes."

"Jesus!" Gallina said in disgust.

McKitrick said, "We'll take the kid in with us. This won't take long."

He started in the closet. Pulled out a pair of heavy work shoes, blobbed and sprayed with a dozen colors. Gallina shook out a pillow on the bed and dropped the shoes into the pillow case.

Gallina had turned to the dresser. He opened a drawer, whistled and pulled out a garish green cardigan with gold buttons, then a tan fringed shawl. He let it fall open to reveal a picture of a pier and blue water and the words, "Brighton, England. Playground of the Kings." He shoved it back and yanked out the whole drawer and dumped its contents on the bed. A gold locket glinted. A dog leash. A white lacy handkerchief.

"There's your damned dresser drawer," he told MacKenzie.

He turned to Carrie. "Did you read him his rights?"

"No."

"Do it. Just be sure you're there with your witnesses at nine A.M. We're going to run a lineup before the newspapers get his picture, spread it all around."

Carrie read from her plastic card. The boy mumbled his responses. He didn't raise his eyes. He was so small. He had terrorized a city, given lifelong nightmares to three old women and a lovely child, burned houses down. It should be easy to despise him. Somehow, she couldn't do that anymore.

McKitrick took his arm, told him, "We found your red car in the paint shop down the street. In back, out of sight. Where you kept it when your mother came. Your buddies there will testify."

Carrie said, "How did you find it? I don't even know how you found this room, or got a warrant."

McKitrick said, "His good buddy up in Santa Rosa had a snapshot. The kid standing by the car he'd just painted red. That old Ford. Your little friend Elizabeth knew him right away. There wasn't any doubt. This is the guy that killed her dog."

He led the boy out of the room. Gallina followed with two bulging pillow slips.

Beyond the bulk of the large bodies moving through the narrow hall Carrie saw people she knew on the street, the miscellany of unkempt faces and clothes that came from Goodwill jumble piles. They're like cats, she thought. They aren't looking at me, but they're looking at me. Her legs were wobbly starting down the stairs. She tugged her hat tight on her head. Alkron was right. That stiffened up her legs. But her nose throbbed and her mouth and cheek were smarting. Roger and MacKenzie followed her, moving past the lab people climbing up to do the room. In the second-floor lobby, more of the faces she'd come to know in her months on these streets.

She paused at the bottom, let the front door slam against the bedlam of fires and fire-fighting. Mackenzie was beside her. "You mangled all the rules, but you found him. You survived," he said. "Those are the important rules." He gently raised her chin to look at her bleeding cheek.

"I didn't see a ring. Probably a fingernail." He had that grave look in his eyes, behind his smile. "Hospital, I think, Roger. This needs a surgeon. I wouldn't want to see a scar there twenty years from now. Even honorably earned."

The words slipped past her. She was looking instead into his face. She would hear them later.

"My car's probably boxed in by fire engines," Roger said.

"Take mine. It's at the corner." MacKenzie pulled out his keys.

Then he turned and pushed the door open and let in the sound and stink of fire. He almost had to shout. "Come back here when you're through!"

He waved his hand out at the street.

"A dozen fires in five buildings. We need witnesses to every step he took. Come back and talk to your street friends. I want signed statements. Wherever they go from here, we'll give them postcards to mail back with their addresses. Tell them we'll pay for airline tickets to bring them back for trial. We'll pay for their hotel rooms. I want him convicted on every fire. Tell them that."

Carrie glanced down the street.

"No bodies," MacKenzie said. "We got everybody out. Firemen searched every room. So did we. Every closet."

He turned and walked down the street. She watched him striding into all that mess of hoses hard with water, a lurid scene illuminated by red flashing lights, an insane world of arching streams of water and roiling dirty smoke, men with blackened faces and dripping chins and fire hats.

Roger gripped her elbow, urged her toward the black and white car parked in the middle of the intersection. He pulled open the door but she turned again to look back down that street.

"It'll all be here when we get back," Roger said.

He looked back, too, at all that mess, and said, "So will MacKenzie."